A Portrait
of Love

ADVANCE PRAISE FOR THE BOOK

'Gautam Choubey's introduction recreates the persona of the iconoclast writer refusing to be cowed down by authority, whether literary or political. It traverses through the times of the poet with amazing insight, anecdotes and references, helping us understand what made "Nirala" so very *nirala*, the inimitable. Choubey's nuanced translation shines a light on Nirala's tryst with language and on his pioneering experiments that shaped the craft of writing in Hindi'—Alka Saraogi

'Nirala is, in my view, the greatest Hindi poet of the twentieth century. As Choubey points out in his introduction, Nirala was also a wonderfully versatile writer of prose. Choubey presents English readers with some of Nirala's stories that are path-breaking both in content and in style'—Ruth Vanita

'Gautam Choubey offers an engrossing translation of selected short stories by Nirala, as well as of Nirala's novella *Billesur Bakriha*, whose satirical exploration of caste and socio-economic realities remains highly topical. This collection of fiction by one of Hindi's greatest writers, accompanied by an erudite introduction, is a welcome addition to the world of translated literature'—Tabish Khair

'Nirala's vivid sketches of life in rural and small-town India before Independence draw a darkly hilarious portrait of a world changing as modernity creeps into traditional communities. They tell compelling stories of survival in a harsh, unforgiving world subjected to a relentlessly unsentimental scrutiny. Nirala's characters engage in desperate manoeuvres to cope with scheming and hostile neighbours, outwit complacent hypocrites, puncture the pomposity of deluded hedonists, and ingeniously negotiate with narrow and rigid social and religious constraints. Delightfully irreverent and irrepressibly playful, Nirala deftly employs pungent humour as social critique and sharp-edged irony as a powerful mode of moral evaluation'—Jatindra K. Nayak

A Portrait *of* Love

SIX STORIES, ONE NOVELLA

Suryakant Tripathi 'Nirala'

Translated from the Hindi by
GAUTAM CHOUBEY

PENGUIN BOOKS
An imprint of Penguin Random House

PENGUIN BOOKS

USA | Canada | UK | Ireland | Australia
New Zealand | India | South Africa | China | Singapore

Penguin Books is part of the Penguin Random House group of companies
whose addresses can be found at global.penguinrandomhouse.com

Published by Penguin Random House India Pvt. Ltd
4th Floor, Capital Tower 1, MG Road,
Gurugram 122 002, Haryana, India

First published in Penguin Books by Penguin Random House India 2024

Translation copyright © Gautam Choubey 2024

ISBN 9780143466376

For sale in the Indian Subcontinent only

Typeset in Adobe Caslon Pro by MAP Systems, Bengaluru, India
Printed at Replika Press Pvt. Ltd, India

www.penguin.co.in

Contents

Introduction   vii

Short Stories   1

    Sukul's Wife   3

    Jyotirmayee   29

    Portrait of a Lady-Love   43

    What I Saw   65

    Chaturi Chamar   87

    Devi   106

Billesur Bakriha   123

Acknowledgements   221

Introduction

Being 'Nirala'

Suryakant Tripathi 'Nirala' (1896–1961) was a Hindi poet, editor and storyteller, often hailed as the greatest exponent of the neo-romantic Chhayavad poetry.[*] His life and writings echo the tragedies, the anguish and the occasional triumphs that marked life in the India of his time. For readers, such echoes acquire tremendous significance, particularly in the works of a bohemian writer like Nirala, whose days of grinding poverty and fabled generosity have both been subjects of national lore, often to the point of eclipsing his literary genius. Mahadevi Verma's

---

[*] David Ruben, arguing after Ram Vilas Sharma, suggests 1899 as the year of Nirala's birth. But I have stuck to 1896, since it is mentioned in a monograph that bears Nirala's handwritten endorsement, suggesting that the poet approved of the year. The year was also verified by Vivek Nirala, Nirala's grandson. See Gangaprasad Pandeya, *Mahapran Nirala* (Prayag: Sahityakar Sansad, 1949).

(1907–87) oft-cited recollection of Nirala 'Bhai' sums up the poet's struggle to find moderation in life. Given how the personal and the literary were nearly indistinguishable in Nirala—a point discussed at some length later in this introduction—the episode begs reiteration.

Once, having somehow come into possession of Rs 300, Nirala entrusted the money to Verma and demanded a budget be drawn up, so he could ration out his monthly expenses. Verma, not particularly penny-wise herself, obliged him with an expenditure plan worked out to the last details. And for once, Nirala's finances looked sorted. But the regime barely lasted a week. 'The very next morning,' writes Verma, 'he came demanding fifty rupees: "There is this student who needs to deposit an exam fee immediately or he'll be debarred from the exams." By sunset, he had to loan out sixty rupees to a fellow writer. The next day, he needed forty rupees to be money-ordered to a tongawallah's mother in Lucknow. And by the afternoon, contributing a hundred rupees to cover the wedding expenses of a deceased friend's niece had become imperative.'[*] It is tempting to suggest that such recklessness in Nirala, both with purse and pen, was prompted by many factors—by his compassionate heart, his love for good literature, the company he kept, the injured pride of an irate poet and, sometimes, by the mere thrill of it all.

---

[*] Mahadevi Verma, 'Nirala Bhai: Jo Rekhayen Na Kah Sakengi', *Path Ke Sathi* (Delhi: Radhakrishna Prakashan, 1956).

'Main Kavi Ho Chala Tha':* Bengal, Tagore and Nirala's Early Life

Nirala was born in 1896 to Ramsahay Tripathi, then an employee of the Mahishadal Raj in Midnapore but originally from Gadhakola in the Bainswari region, Kannauj. Owing to the circumstances of his birth—born on a Sunday and to a mother devoted to the Sun god—he was fondly named Suryakumar, which he later changed to Suryakant.

Nirala's education began in a Bengali-medium village school, followed by some years at the Mahishadal Raj High School, where he was exposed to English. In the absence of a formal introduction to Hindi, his engagement with the language was mediated through *Ramcharitmanas* and *Braj Vilas*, which he read recreationally, mostly in the company of the Bainswari diaspora employed at the Mahishadal estate. He thus received his early education with Bengali as his first language and Sanskrit as his second. Football, swimming, wrestling, musical soirées and members of the royal family to keep him company—life offered all the excitements a boy his age could wish for. However, when he failed his high school matriculation exam and his hitherto doting father banished him from home, he sought refuge at his wife's ancestral home in Dalmau, Raebareli. This was in 1914, two years after his marriage to Manohara Devi, a perceptive woman with a refined literary taste.

---

* See 'Sukul's Wife' in this volume. Here, Nirala reminisces how he had become a poet of sorts very early in his life.

Some even suggest that the young Suryakant failed his exam on purpose, to match the erudition of Rabindranath Tagore (1861–1941); since Tagore had received no formal education, Nirala could not risk matriculating. Even though the two never met, Nirala formed a complex relationship with Gurudeb. During his days in Calcutta, he once picked up a bitter feud with Ilachandra Joshi (1903–82)—the pioneering novelist who brought psychological realism to Hindi letters—when the latter suggested that Tagore's poetry, on account of his exposure to world literature, was superior even to that of Kalidas (fifth century CE) and Mira (1498–1547). Nirala harboured a mostly unvoiced rivalry with Tagore, often calling attention to the idea that class privilege may have unfairly added to Tagore's literary renown. He nevertheless remained an ardent admirer of Tagore's craft. Of the two monographs he wrote on fellow poets, his first, *Ravindra Kavita Kanan* (1928), is a critical study of Tagore's poetry.

Be that as it may, the next three years in Dalmau were productive and educative for Nirala. It was here that both his children were born—Ramkrishna in 1914 and Saroj in 1917. Further, at the prodding of his wife, who awakened him to his limited knowledge of Khari Boli, he embarked on a mission to improve his Hindi.[*] To this end, he took to studying the previous issues of *Saraswati* (1900) and *Maryada* (1909), comparing closely Hindi grammar with

---

[*] In the autobiographical novel *Kulli Bhat* (1939), Nirala provides a humbling confession of his inadequacies in Hindi and his subsequent grind to master it.

that of Bengali, English and Sanskrit, and taking Mahavir Prasad Dwivedi (1864–1938) as his guru in absentia. It was also during this exile that he composed his first significant poem, 'Juhi Ki Kali' (Jasmine Bud).

By 1917, Nirala had mastered four languages—Bengali, Sanskrit, Hindi and English—each of which he harnessed judiciously in his works. With his deep knowledge of Bengali, he made quick money translating the novels of Bankimchandra into Hindi, albeit anonymously; with his complete mastery over Sanskrit, he excelled as the editor of the Ramakrishna Mission's Vedanta-based periodical *Samanvay* (1922), impressing the Calcutta-based writers with his grasp over the scriptures; with his command over Khari Boli, he fashioned a new idiom in Hindi, liberating poetry from the iron grip of rhymed metre and introducing bold new themes in prose; with his easy familiarity with English, he assailed literary opponents, including his formidable foe Banarasidas Chaturvedi (1892–1985).[*] According to linguist Udaynarayan Tiwari (1903–84), Nirala could easily switch between languages to suit his mood. 'When in high spirits, Nirala spoke his mother tongue, Bainswari. A conversation in Bengali, too, meant a happy disposition, since it was also a mother tongue to him. But at the faintest bout of anger, he would switch to a highly Sanskritized register of Hindi. And when ragingly furious, he spoke only in English.'[†]

His prose pieces included in this volume exhibit a similar linguistic variety—from the Sanskritized Hindi

---

[*] See 'Pandit Banarasidas Ka Angrezi Gyan', *Sudha*, May 1935.

[†] Kailash Chandra Bhatia, 'Nirala Ki Bhasha', *Kavyatma Nirala*, n.d.

of 'Devi' to the Urdu-mixed Hindi of 'Nayika Parichay' ('Portrait of a Lady-Love'), and from copious use of the Bainswari dialect in *Billesur Bakriha* to the generous sprinkling of English in 'Sukul Ki Biwi' ('Sukul's Wife'). Likewise, his writings also abound in references, motifs, loanwords and playful appropriations—sometimes well-known, sometimes obscure—from a wide range of resources. These include Sanskrit mantras and shlokas, couplets from *Ramcharitmanas*, biting provincial proverbs, Perso–Arabic legends, accounts of contemporary feuds (both literary and political), anecdotes and music.[*]

In a Doordarshan documentary on Nirala, eminent progressive critic Ram Vilas Sharma (1912–2000) draws attention to the poet's erudition. 'It must be emphasized,' argues Sharma, 'that Nirala was one of the greatest scholars of his time. While people sing paeans to his poetic genius, they somehow overlook how very learned a man he was.'[†] In a certain sense, it is this formidable erudition which makes reading and translating him a daunting challenge. The present selection bears testimony to the density and frequency of allusions in Nirala's prose. Such allusions serve living reference points within the fabric of the story, rather than mere markers of pedantry, sophistry or erudition. From the Panchatantra and obscure wedding customs to the intrigues of world history, and from ancient

---

[*] Nirala was a man with considerable musical talent. Impressed with his vocal skills, the raja of Mahishadal estate had even made arrangements for his training in music.

[†] Prasar Bharti Archives (21 February 2020), *Mahakavi: Suryakant Tripathi Nirala*, YouTube.

philosophical feuds to contemporary controversies—
everything fuses seamlessly in Nirala's prose, connecting
readers to the world beyond his literary cosmos and setting
modern translators on a wild goose chase as they falter to
identify the references.

'Dukh Heen Jeewan Ki Katha Rahi':[*]
A Man of Sorrows

In the story 'Sukul's Wife', included in this volume, Nirala
offers a passing account of his self-education in Dalmau.
However, his days of peaceful learning came to a rude end
in 1917 with the sudden death of his father. He was now
an orphan, having lost his mother at the age of three. But
this was not the end of his tragedy. In 1918, a year later,
he lost his wife, his cousin and his sister-in-law to the
influenza epidemic.

For all the adulation and notoriety Nirala came to
command, death and suffering seem to have been the only
constants in his life. Later, in 1935, when his nineteen-year-
old daughter died, evidently due to privation, Nirala penned
a *shok kavya* or elegy titled 'Saroj Smriti' (Remembrance
of Saroj), considered one of the most poignant verse
compositions in Khari Boli.[†] Intensely personal in tone,
the 159 rhyming couplets of the poem offer an intimate
portrait of the dead daughter and are a sad admission of
the poet's failure to support his family even as he waged a

---

[*] From 'Saroj Smriti', published in the anthology *Anamika* (1938) along
with 'Ram Ki Shakti Puja'.

[†] Ibid.

high-pitched battle against the rot in society and literature. The poem ends with a lament that sums up Nirala's life:

> My life has been a saga of sorrows,
> What more could I say today that I haven't said by now?[*]

One may surmise that by the time Nirala's literary career took off, he was already a lonely and broken man. With a long life that lay ahead and six children to support—two of his own and four his cousin's—it was his love of literature that helped him stay afloat. Throughout his life, Nirala refused to surrender in the face of mounting difficulties, whether caused by personal sorrows, hurtful critics or his own reckless ways; he sought solace in literature and scoffed at the tragedies with humour, satire and poetry.

This is particularly evident in 'Ram Ki Shakti Puja' (Ram Worships Shakti, 1935), composed shortly after Saroj's death—an incident that marked the lowest ebb in Nirala's life. Weaving together features of epic narrative, plot elements from Krittibas Ojha's (1381–1461) *Sriram Panchaali* and the religiosity of Bengal's Shakti cult, the poem shows Ram rising from the abyss of despair to slay Ravan. Likewise, in 'Tulisdas' (1938), Nirala celebrates a poetic life marred by early setbacks and filial conflicts until its final ascent to the summit of glory. In a sense, the two narratives allegorize Nirala's own will to prevail in the face of adversities and tragic misfortunes. This was also the time he turned more resolutely to prose fiction, publishing the short-story collection *Lilly* in 1933, the

---

[*] Ibid.

very jovial *Nirupama* in 1936 and the autobiographical *Kulli Bhat* in 1939.

Writing for the Nirala memorial issue of *Aaj* (29 October 1961), socialist critic Chandrabali Singh (1924–2011) argued: 'Nirala's realist prose writings, much like his poetry, reflect a persona that remains undaunted in the midst of adversities.' Each of Nirala's 'heroes' in the present selection displays the same fortitude and undaunted spirit that one finds in Nirala's own temperament. In 'Chaturi Chamar', it is palpable in the poor tanner's stoic resolve to fight a hopeless legal battle against the mighty zamindar; in *Billesur Bakriha*, it can be seen in the friendless goatherd's determination to thrive in a cruel, dog-eat-dog village; in 'Sukul's Wife', it echoes clearly in an enterprising woman's audacity to marry a man of her choice, even if it invites the wrath of her own people; in 'Jyotirmayee', it is unmissable in a widow's belief that nothing in God's universe can thwart her pursuit of happiness; in 'Devi', it takes the form of the stoic indifference that a mute beggar woman puts on, finding solace only in her child and conversing silently with it.

'Jab Top Mukabil Hai, Toh Akhbar Nikalo':[*]
From Calcutta to Allahabad

Nirala's earliest publication was a comparative study of the grammars of Bengali and Hindi. It appeared in 1916 in

---

[*] Vishnuchandra Sharma, 'Patrakar Nirala', *Sahitya Devta Nirala* (Jaipur: Rachna Prakashan: 1970), p. 75.

Saraswati, a periodical which had also famously rejected the much-lauded 'Juhi Ki Kali' (Jasmine Bud). Later, in 1922, at the recommendation of Mahavir Prasad Dwivedi, the editor of the very same monthly, Nirala moved to Calcutta and began editing the Ramakrishna Mission's periodical *Samanvay*. However, it was during his two-year association with the hallowed 'Matwala Mandal'—as the coterie of writers and journalists involved with the satirical weekly *Matwala* (1923–30) came to be lionized—that Nirala cemented his position in the literary circuit.

With an editorial board comprising the likes of Shivpujan Sahay (1893–1963), Mahadev Prasad Seth (d. 1963), Navjadiklal Shrivastav (1852–1932) and, later, Pandey Bechan Sharma 'Ugra' (1900–67), *Matwala* sparked a new wave of creativity, particularly in political satire, reportage and poetry. Even though the fast-burgeoning Hindi public sphere was being served judiciously by periodicals like *Saraswati*, *Pratap* (1913) and *Madhuri* (1921), the space for satire and humour had shrunk since the days of Bharatendu Harischandra (1850–85) and Balmukund Gupta (1865–1907). Published by the Balkrishna Press of Calcutta and housed in the same building as *Samanvay*, *Matwala* filled this vacuum with rare panache, commanding a formidable circulation figure of 10,000 within the first year of its publication. The weekly mounted a no-holds-barred critique of the incongruities of caste, community, religion, language, literature and, above all, the injustices of colonial administration. Besides, it also undertook to instruct readers in the matters of *ruchi*, or taste, emboldening them to be active seekers of facts and perspectives. As for its motto, *Matwala* proclaimed:

What use wielding a longbow, why swing a dagger?
When up against a fearsome cannon, print a paper.[*]

It was indeed *Matwala* that gave free rein to the poet in Nirala, also publishing the previously snubbed 'Juhi Ki Kali' in its eighth issue. Debunking traditional prosody and end rhyme, Nirala fashioned a new, vivacious poetic idiom with his first published anthology in 1923, suitably titled *Anamika*, or that which is beyond naming. All of twenty-six years, Nirala chaperoned the weekly's poetry segment, copy-edited submissions, writing pseudonymously drew daggers against the literary giants of the age, and took on the penname 'Nirala' to rhyme with *Matwala*.

However, after an enthralling year with *Matwala*, creative differences surfaced. Nirala broke away from the weekly but continued to live in Calcutta, eking out a living by translating, editing books and writing commissioned biographies. In 1927, following a prolonged illness, he decided to convalesce in Banaras and hung about the city for several months. In 1928, he moved to Lucknow and began working for Dulare Lal Bhargav's (1900–75) Ganga Pustakalay. Over the next fourteen years, the mysticism of Nirala's Chhayavadi idiom matured further, imbuing his imagination with greater audacity and his language with a striking directness. Perhaps, the 1938 poetry anthology

---

[*] Ibid.

Anamika—a revised and expanded version of his debut anthology—was the crowning achievement of this phase. Reveling in the virtuosity of an idiom liberated from the recondite rules of both prosody and prose, Nirala draws strikingly realist portraits, particularly of those on the periphery, and subjects them to a fresh gaze. In the much-anthologized poem 'Wah Todti Patthar' (She Splits Stones), included in *Anamika,* he extols a woman labourer's beauty and toughness, instead of pitying her hard life. In prose, too, he breaks free from progressive literature's tendency to treat its subjects with pathos. In the short story 'Devi', the narrator feels both smitten and humbled by the sight of a mute beggar woman. 'Not even the greatest of poets,' declaims the narrator, 'would've fathomed her voiceless majesty, or pictured a form and bearing so exceptional as hers.'

According to Walter Rubin, this phase is also characterized by a 'much franker preoccupation with actual circumstances of the poet's own life'.[*] In fact, so compelling are the similarities between his life and works that one may attempt an intellectual biography of Nirala by just following his writings and the order of their appearance. We see him not just doing literature, but, in fact, living it. In other words, he looks at literature through life, and at life through literature. This also explains the penchant for self-reflexivity that characterizes stories included in this volume, all of which, with the exception of 'Kya Dekha' ('What I Saw'), were written during his Lucknow days.

---

[*] Walter Rubin, 'Nirala and the Renaissance of Hindi Poetry', *Journal of Asian Studies*, vol. 31, no. 1, November 1971, pp. 111–26.

In 1943, Nirala relocated to Allahabad and stayed there till the end of his life. In between, he also worked with the Unnao-based Yug Mandir, first in 1943 and then during 1945–47. Several accounts suggest that Nirala suffered a mental breakdown and bouts of schizophrenia during the last decade of his life. Whatever be the truth, he continued to be prolific, publishing consummate anthologies that point to mental vigour and clarity of thought.

'Isilye Meri Kadra Nahi Hui':* An Author in Search of Friends, Enemies and Publishers

Nirala was outgoing and an extrovert. Possessing natural charm in abundance, he quickly made friends who stood him in good stead. In Banaras, he befriended Premchand (1880–1936), Jaishankar Prasad (1889–1937) and Vinod Shankar Vyas (1903–68); in Lucknow, he formed close ties with Amritlal Nagar (1916–90), Ram Vilas Sharma and Shrinarayan Chaturvedi (1895–1990); in Allahabad, he bonded affectionately with Mahadevi Verma. With his quirks, foibles and peculiarities of appearance—that swung between being overdressed and bare-bodied—Nirala left such a deep impression on the people he met that nearly all his contemporaries have written about their experience of meeting him. However, from Banaras to Allahabad, no community of writers could remotely match the short-lived vibrancy of Calcutta's 'Matwala Mandal'.

---

* See 'Devi', included in this anthology.

The template of literary collaborations that flourished till the 1920s—centred on editors like Bhartendu Harischandra and Mahavir Prasad Dwivedi, and organizations like Nagri Pracharini Sabha (1893, Banaras) and Hindi Sahitya Sammelan (1911, Allahabad)—was driven by the imperatives of the Hindi movement. These included systematizing studies of Hindi, introducing new genres to the world of Hindi letters, promoting academic research, drawing a credible ancestry of the language and publishing textbooks. *Matwala* contributed its bit to the movement by addressing the rather risky question of literary taste in Hindi.

However, by the 1930s, the sweeping force of language activism had waned, and the world of Hindi letters had graduated to addressing the issues of themes and style.[*] Even though the Hindi public sphere's nationalist charge was still strong, the ideological positions—anchored to both politics and aesthetics—were quickly hardening. For a rebel like Nirala, who rejected all manner of indoctrinations and called out duplicity wherever he sensed it, the ever-polarizing world of Hindi literature became a slippery terrain to tread on. And he often grumbled about his own solitude. In 'Devi', Nirala reflects dolefully on his idealism-wrought-isolation and writes: 'Now I see why I never garnered much respect, why I suffered such privation . . . the more I tried to uplift society through my writings, the harder it tried to pull me down.'

---

[*] See Gautam Choubey's PhD thesis: *Hindi Prose and Gandhian First Principles: Issues of Community, Agency and Justice (1915–1948).*

Part of his loneliness also stemmed from his tendency to rake up and nurture rivalries. The long-running tussle between Nirala and Banarasidas Chaturvedi, which repeatedly spilt out in public with vitriolic overtones, is among the most notorious literary feuds of the Hindi world. Among other points of contention, Nirala accused Chaturvedi of abusing his proximity to Gandhi and Tagore to humiliate literary rivals. But it seems Nirala himself didn't take too kindly to criticism either. Peeved by Sumitranandan Pant's (1900–77) well-meaning critique of his poetry, he offered a hundred-page rejoinder in *Pant Aur Pallav*.* In return, Pant—once a close friend and a fellow Chhayavadi—never paid Nirala a visit, even though they both lived out their days in Allahabad. Likewise, when Premchand's protégé Bhuwaneshwar (1910–57)—proclaimed as the 'future' of Hindi at the Progressive Writers' Conference in 1936—wrote a piece critical of Chhayavad, Nirala was quick to return the favour, even denigrating the young littérateur as *awaara*, or a ruffian. Since Nirala wielded considerable influence in literary circles, it was difficult to make light of his censure. For some, the consequences were a little too debilitating. Bhuwaneshwar was rattled by Nirala's attack, and his literary career tragically nosedived.†

But Nirala saw his criticism, however strongly worded, as essential to the progress of Hindi literature. The publisher's note to *Prabandh Pratima* (1940), a

---

* Vishwambhar Manav, *Kavya Ka Devta: Nirala* (Allahabad: Lokbharti Publication, 1969), p. 23.

† Doodnath Singh (ed.), *Bhuvaneshwar Samagra* (New Delhi: Rajkamal Prakashan, 2012).

collection of Nirala's essays, suggests that although a few pieces in the book are critical of leading political and literary figures of the day, students of literature may find them useful because 'all truthful accounts of the progress of literature include such essays too'.[*] Nirala's own preface to the anthology offers a heartfelt apology, suggesting he could not be 'decorous' at all places, and that readers may come across instances of 'ignorance, arrogance and even unliterariness' in the essays. However, in the interest of literature, and to make certain his own weaknesses did not go unnoticed either, he would not tinker one bit with the content of the essays or blunt their sharp tenor.[†]

Nonetheless, the narratorial voice in Nirala is deeply sympathetic to those in the profession of writing. The narrator is often a poet/writer/journalist himself, struggling to keep his body and soul together. This makes his writings both autobiographical and journalistic, with the author as an empathetic eyewitness to the world he portrays. Like a print historian, Nirala extensively chronicles the business of writing and selling books in his time—a quality that makes his work stand out among his contemporaries. His fictional universe teems with impoverished writers, miserly publishers, indifferent readers and spiteful critics. Every now and then, one comes across a poet lamenting rejection by a weekly's editor, or a novelist advised by his publisher to write something that titillates and therefore sells. In most cases, the seething littérateur is Nirala himself. The literary

---

[*] Suryakant Tripathi Nirala, *Prabandh Pratima* (Allahabad: Leader Press, 1940).

[†] Ibid.

world emerges as a character in these pieces, rather than merely a shaping background.

The relationship between market forces and art remains a perennial concern, both in Nirala's writings and his life. Several of Nirala's pieces speak poignantly of his stubborn attempts at keeping his vision of art aloft in the capital-driven world of print. Although Nirala's literary crusade never quite gathers the momentum he would have liked, his idealism was put through a particularly trying phase during World War II. With an administrative clampdown on press freedom and an acute scarcity of printing paper, most of the literary publications shut their operations, pushing writers to the brink of penury and starvation. Nirala lived in Daraganj, Allahabad, at the time; he endured unspeakable hardships and had to make impossible sacrifices to keep his literary beacon aglow. In the words of Gangaprasad Pandey:

> Seeing Nirala roam about the streets of Prayag—barefooted, bareheaded, cloaked in tattered kurta and soiled dhoti, sometimes barely reaching the knees—one's heart sank in despair. He would walk all the way from Daraganj to Indian Press and Leader Press, carrying his poems for publication. Truth be told, the miseries Nirala braved from 1943 to 1946 would have surely driven another to suicide.[*]

---

[*] Gangaprasad Pandey, *Mahapran Nirala* (Prayag: Sahityakar Sansad, 1949), p. 102.

The fact that Nirala had also sold off all his copyrights made things worse for him. Yet he remained steadfast in his idealism, holding his own against preying booksellers, composing and publishing two poetry collections—*Naye Patte* and *Bela*—in 1946.

'. . . Brahman Samaj Mein Jyon Achhut':[*]
Feasting on the Forbidden

In his study of Nirala's life and poetry, Vishwambhar 'Manav' takes strong exception to how fellow writers and critics often singled out his food habits and addictions for censure, as if no other littérateur consumed meat or alcohol:

> In their respective memoirs, Dr Udaynarayan Tiwari speaks of his cigarette addiction, Ugra and Bedhab Banarasi take note of his fondness for bhang-laced drinks, Upendranath Ashk points to his love for meat, and Vinod Shankar Vyas writes about his drinking habits.[†]

It is not usual for an author's personal life to be put through the same rigorous scrutiny as his writings; facts of biography are limited to education, family, literary influences and the occasional spell of autobiographical elements in their writings. However, with Nirala, every aspect of the personal

---

[*] From the poem 'Hindi Ke Sumano Ke Prati', see *Nirala, Nirala Sanchayita*, ed. Rameshchandra Shah (New Delhi: Vani Prakashan, 2010), p. 115.

[†] Vishwambhar Manav, *Kavya Ka Devta: Nirala*, p. 22.

is the literary. His choice of attire, his decision to get rid of the Brahminical tuft, his involvement in body-building and even his style of wearing facial hair—all codified a mostly well-thought-out public persona. Similarly, bhang and non-vegetarian food epitomized his penchant for subverting Brahminical norms, particularly those relating to pollution and purity.

In many of his stories, we find an autobiographical narrator proclaim aloud his love for meat, without the slightest care for his good name in the community. In 'Chaturi Chamar', the narrator demands a regular supply of fresh meat as the 'guru dakshina' for tutoring Chaturi's son. The supply is then cooked and consumed with some pomp in the company of people considered untouchable by upper-caste Hindus. Likewise, in 'Sukul's Wife', when asked if he eats chicken, the narrator says: 'as a matter of principle.' In fact, as an immediate response to his literary dispute with Gandhi, the context of which is discussed later in this essay, Nirala penned a poem titled 'Bapu Ke Prati' (For Bapu):

> Bapu, if you ate chicken,
> Would you still be worshipped
> By all and sundry?
> Would these many Hindi writers–poets have kneeled to you,
> Head over heels in devotion?[*]

In the poem, eating chicken provides an enabling context for a candid reassessment of Gandhi's sainthood, particularly

---

[*] *Nirala Sanchayita*, ed. Rameshchandra Shah, p. 122.

among the Hindi literati. Writing for the August 1930 issue of *Sudha*, Nirala undertakes an exhaustive exploration of ethical and practical issues with meat-eating in an article plainly titled 'Niramish', or vegetarian. Even though he concludes by proclaiming vegetarianism to be the superior eating habit, the essay upholds a clear preference for expediency over dogmatic compliance. 'While I consider it *rajasik*, catering mostly to sensual gratification,' argues Nirala, 'freshly cooked meat gives more nutrition than stale chapattis. It is the right food for regular people, caught in the grind for survival.'

Nirala launched a blistering critique of all things sacrosanct. However, instead of offering a bird's-eye view of the socio-cultural landscapes, he studied the local, tracing patterns of percolation, localization and (mis) appropriations. Consequently, his politics, too, became deeply personal. His penchant for subversive conduct find expression in everyday practices. In the stories included in this book, Nirala writes about dining without inhibitions, coupled with a Brahmin's fondness for non-vegetarian food—his way of undermining regressive traditions.

Likewise, through the theme of forbidden love, that permeates several of his stories, he mounts a trenchant attack on patriarchy. His female characters—imbued with agency, resourcefulness, resilience and courage—trifle with the forces of patriarchy in ways that catches everyone unawares. In 'Portrait of a Lady-love', a man-about-town is repeatedly tricked by a much younger college girl; In 'What I Saw', a courtesan takes charge in the wooing game and does the chasing; in 'Jyotiramyee', a young widow resorts to a clever ploy to humble a disappointingly conservative 'modern' man.

However, it needs to be emphasized that Nirala's iconoclasm was not limited to his person; in an era of stifling orthodoxies, his gestures of defiance echoed the collective cry for change. In the poem 'Jaldi Jaldi Pair Badhao, Aao, Aao,' (Come, Be Quick on Your Feet) Nirala calls for a revolutionary reordering of society—so that 'the proud mansions of the rich shall serve as schools for the poor' and the onus to dispel the darkness shall lie with the 'Dhobi, Pasi, Chamar, Teli'. Commenting on Nirala's prose fiction, noted critic Jatindra Kumar Nayak observes that the stories—with their unpolished realism and a strong autobiographical strain—chronicle the winds of change as they slowly but surely swept through society. And in each instance, these changes were championed by those on the socio-economic periphery. In the poem 'Hindi Ke Sumano Ke Prati' (For the Luminaries of Hindi), Nirala calls himself *vasant ka agradoot*, or the messenger of spring, who had to live like an untouchable among the Brahmins ('*Brahman samaj mein jyon achhut*').[*] In *Billesur Bakriha*, a Brahmin goatherd's final triumph is aided by the downtrodden of his village.

'. . . Isliye Samarpan Sthagit Karta Hoon':[†] Gandhi, Nehru and an Angry Poet

If modernity is about realizing a consciousness mediated by an individual's experiences, Nirala was a true modernist.

---

[*] https://www.hindwi.org/kavita/hindi-ke-sumnon-ke-prati-patr-surykant-tripathi-nirala-kavita

[†] Nirala, *Kulli Bhat* (Lucknow: Ganga Granthagar, 1939).

And since experiences cannot be patterned or homogenized, one also encounters occasional contradictions in his thoughts. However, at a time when nearly every writer subscribed to one or more of the dominant ideologies, Nirala stubbornly resisted indoctrination, scoffing at the follies of each without exception. In the satirical fable 'Kukurmutta' (1942), a kukurmutta, or the common Indian mushroom, launches a scathing attack on a rose, a veritable privileged capitalist, asserting its own utility and, therefore, superiority over the latter:

> Now, listen well, you pathetic rose,
> Don't forget, to possess that fragrance, that colour bright,
> You've ravaged the poor manure: you impolite!
> A thoroughgoing capitalist, posing boastfully on a stem,
> You've had the gardener weather biting chill and scorching sun.[*]

If capitalism is Western in origin, the socialist Nehru—as Nirala reminds the readers in the poem 'Mahangu' (Man of Expensive Taste)—is a 'London graduate' and a friend to the foreigners. In the poem 'Van Bela' (1938), Nirala ridicules a magnate's need to posture as a firebrand communist and preach revolution while clinging hypocritically to his wealth. To Nirala, public posturing and crafty speeches were not enough to help the cause of the oppressed. In *Billesur Bakriha*, 'Devi' and 'Chaturi Chamar', Nirala seems to suggest that it is possible, even desirable, to empathize with the poor without embracing doctrinal Marxism.

---

[*] *Nirala Sanchayita*, p. 128.

The satire in 'Van Bela' doesn't stop with the aforementioned exposé. Nirala goes on to show how a socialist impostor is being praised to the skies by the world of Hindi letters—first by those who compose poems in his honour and then by those who declare the poems to be masterpieces. Nirala cringed at the servile bond the Hindi literati formed with politics, particularly with those leaders who were vested in the promotion of Hindi. Since the flourishing of Hindi print culture was catalyzed by the nationalist movement, its relationship with politics was reduced largely to reciprocity; the champions of the nation, who also championed Hindi, were to be extolled by Hindi writers and editors. In return, Hindi activists expected writers to ceremonially embrace their activities— by 'blessing' Hindi conferences with their chairmanships or presidential addresses, publishing articles on Hindi and occasionally writing a preface to a Hindi textbook. The cases of Bharatiya Sahitya Sammelan (1935) and the Pragatisheel Lekhak Sangh (1936)—both envisaged as forums to bring regional literature to the national (read Hindi) mainstream—illustrate the point well.

In 1935, during the Indore convention of the Bharatiya Sahitya Sammelan, a blueprint for a pan-Indian literary association was prepared under the supervision of Gandhi. Although K.M. Munshi (1887–1971) had floated the idea a decade earlier, it wasn't until the Mahatma 'blessed' it with his chairmanship that the plan took off. In an article published in the November 1935 issue of *Hans*, Premchand expressed a profound sense of validation upon learning that Nehru's views on the need to unite provincial literatures concurred with those of Gandhi and the Sammelan.

Later, for the chairmanship of the Pragatisheel Lekhak Sangh, Nehru was Premchand's first choice. While Nirala did acknowledge the contributions of Gandhi and Nehru to India, he had no qualms about attacking them whenever they judged Hindi too harshly or indiscreetly. During the aforementioned conference in Indore, Gandhi had condescendingly suggested that Hindi lacked a writer of Rabindranath's calibre. Later, while in Lucknow, Nirala made him eat his words. 'I barely know anything of Hindi,' Gandhi had to concede.[*]

'It seems you're less concerned whether there are Hindi writers with Rabindranath's literary genius and more keen to find a grandson of Prince Dwarkanath Thakur or a Nobel laureate,' concluded Nirala during the twenty-minute-long meeting, leaving Gandhi speechless.

As someone who truly believed in the expressive resources of Hindi, Nirala could not stomach half-baked or ill-informed assessments of its literature. He also fought for the respect he felt was due to Hindi writers. Once, on his way to Calcutta from Lucknow, he barged into the second-class train carriage that carried Nehru and assailed him with a battery of questions and criticism. Nirala grumbled that while Subhas Chandra Bose (1897–1945) had remembered to mourn the death of Sarat Chandra Chattopadhyay (1876–1938) in his presidential address, there was no reference to Jaishankar Prasad in Nehru's address, even though Nehru came from the Hindi region. This, to Nirala, was a measure of

---

[*] *Nirala Rachnawali*, vol. 6 (New Delhi: Rajkamal Prakashan, 1983), p. 215.

Nehru's haughty ignorance. Further, he decried Nehru's pejorative labelling of Banaras-based literati as 'darbari' or courtly, especially when the city boasted committed doyens in all three branches of Hindi letters—Prasad in poetry, Premchand in prose fiction and Ramachandra Shukla (1884–1941) in criticism.

Nirala wasn't content playing second fiddle to political discourses or politicians. As a writer, he wanted a certain measure of autonomy, which meant, among other things, the freedom to critique the national political leadership. Nirala sincerely believed that there were areas where the efficacy of literature was far greater than that of politics. In an essay titled 'Nehru Ji Se Do Baatein' (A Conversation with Nehru), Nirala writes:

> Take, for example, the question of Hindu–Muslim unity; I trust it can be better addressed in the new literature of Hindi than in the political discourses. And the reason is simple: while politics is influenced by Western paradigms, literature flourishes in our native originality.[*]

In the aforementioned episodes, Nirala comes across as a hot-headed, arrogant poet. But it wasn't so much Nirala's vanity as his sensitivity towards Hindi that provoked these confrontations. It also (in)famously prompted him to withhold the custom of dedicating a book in *Kulli Bhat*; since he could not find anyone worthy among the eminences, he announced the ritual as *sthagit*, or deferred.

---

[*] *Nirala Rachnawali*, vol. 6 (New Delhi: Rajkamal Prakashan, 1983), pp. 217–19.

'Nav Gati, Nav Lay, Taal Chhand Nav':* Rethinking Realism in Twentieth-Century Hindi

The astonishing range of Nirala's prose brings to light new ways of engaging with realism in Hindi, also inviting us, inter alia, to reconsider the legacy of the Chhayavadi writers. For far too long now, the domain of Hindu–Urdu literature, as perceived by English readers, is limited to the writings of Saadat Hasan Manto (1912–55), Premchand and Ismat Chugtai (1915–91). Connoisseurs of Hindi novels seldom go beyond translations of Premchand and Yashpal (1903–76). To them, Jaishankar Prasad and Nirala are primarily poets, while Mohan Rakesh (1925–72) is a playwright. The regional novel (*aanchalikupanyas*) is discussed almost exclusively with reference to Phanishwar Nath Renu (1921–77); satire through the writings of Harishankar Parsai (1924–95) and Shrilal Shukla (1925–2011); feminism with Mannu Bhandari (1931–2021); and modernism with reference to Rajendra Yadav (1929–2013). This tapered approach to Hindi literature, on account of the very limited repertoire of translations, has not only been detrimental to the legacy of other major writers but also to the debates they stirred and the issues they championed.

According to Ram Vilas Sharma, Nirala even flattens the old template of plot, driven towards happy endings and resolution.[†] His provocative prose, which blends

---

* https://kavishala.in/sootradhar/suryakant-tripathi-nirala/vara-de-vinavadini

[†] Ram Vilas Sharma, *Nirala Ki Sahitya Saadhan*, vol. 2 (New Delhi: Rajkamal Prakashan, 1981), p. 470.

astute observations of a journalist with the radical idiom of a progressive, invites readers to reconsider the legacy of early- to mid-twentieth-century Hindi prose. Borrowing techniques from many sources, but mostly from his own life experiences, Nirala constantly strives to create something new—a tireless pursuit that defines the motto of his life and writings.

One may call it a happy coincidence that the very learned Nirala was born on Vasant Panchami—a day dedicated to Saraswati, the goddess of learning. In his famous prayer to Saraswati—sung ritually across India on his birthday but generally without remembering its errant composer—his quest for newness finds the clearest expression. In many ways, the song provides a fitting denouement to this introductory essay on Nirala.

> The One who plays veena, pray bless us.
> Bless us, O Veenavadini, bless us,
> With the cherished symphony of freedom, with the
> mantra that yields the elixir of life;
> With these let Bharat be awash,
> Bless us, O Veenavadini, bless us.
>
> A new spur, a new tune, a new rhythm, verses new,
> To man a new language, to the clouds a new music,
> To this new swarm of birds that soars in the new sky,
> Pray give new wings, a new song.
> Bless us, O Veenavadini, bless us.

Short Stories

Sukul's Wife[*]

1

All this happened a long time ago. Back then, I was busy churning the endless ocean of literature, hoping for the elusive life-bestowing nectar. However, my efforts yielded nothing except deadly poisons, with only Mahadev Babu, the editor of *Matwala*, willing to gulp it down, as Lord Shiva once did. He would nudge me on with dreams of discovering a treasure soon enough—precious as rare gems and enchanting like the nymph Rambha—were I to be relentless in my pursuit. Even though the hellfire of literary poisons charred my soul—more than they ever seared Mahadev Babu's—I drew comfort from the fact that he had faith in my abilities, much more than I myself ever had. Leaning on his confidence, I quit my job as the editor of a drab religious magazine, which was fixated on

---

[*] Originally published as 'Sukul Ki Biwi' in a 1941 collection of short stories of the same title.

the Vedanta, and surrendered religiously to the fair maiden called poetry, endlessly colourful in her demeanour.

Fortunately, within a few months, my efforts bore fruit. Describing the episode of Kamdev's incineration by Shiva, Tulsidas writes that for two *dand*, or nearly an hour, Kamdev succeeded in arousing the carnal longings of the entire cosmos; during that span, women saw everything as masculine, and men as feminine. But now, as I take stock of my own state, I find his description somewhat underwhelming. Ever since I began worshipping poetry, the cosmos seems feminine to me all the time—whether dreaming or wide-eyed—except when I'm in a dead slumber.

Just as I was thinking these thoughts, somebody called out my name and asked the doorman, 'Is he home?'

The voice felt like the sound of a veena. As if pleased with my devotion, the nectar-throated goddess of poetry had arrived herself to make inquiries about me, calling out my name with tender affection. A sweet sensation coursed through my body. In that moment, the heroines of Kalidasa, Shakespeare, Bankimchandra and Rabindranath—each one of them flashed before my eyes. I can't say how, but I was somehow sure she was the same beauty—the one I had spotted strolling yesterday, near Cornwallis Square.

Noticing me, she had lowered her gaze. Oh, what lovely eyes she had! Brimming over with tales waiting to be told! Her glorious image had beamed in the guileless mirror of my heart. I, too, had breezed past the maiden nonchalantly, trying to impress it upon her that I was polite, cultured, educated and bore good character too.

As I stepped out of my room, I saw a car parked near the gate. It must be hers, I thought. She must have asked her driver to track me down. And now that she had my name and address, she had come over to meet me. Indeed, she was a student of Bethune College. That was exactly where I had seen her. She must be into poetry too. Perhaps she was here to appreciate my poems better, having previously savoured only a fragment of the liberating charm my verses exude. Since going out to greet her would have diminished my self-esteem, I ordered the gateman to show her in.

Just then, I became painfully aware of my naked torso. Well, I would have surely clothed it, if only I had something to wear. I imagined dressing myself up in all manners of expensive suits, but, in reality, there were only two dirty kurtas close at hand. I felt a seething anger at my publishers. These low-born creatures have no respect for writers. I dashed straight to Munshiji's room, collected his silk shawl and draped it carefully around my neck, trying to judge if it looked good on me. I stayed alert to the approaching sounds, but the stairs had gone quiet. I thought of my hair—what if it's tousled. I grabbed a mirror and, straining my eyes repeatedly, closely examined my face. Survey done, I tucked the mirror under the mattress and put out Shaw's *Getting Married* on display. I was reading it with the help of a dictionary. The dictionary was promptly put out of sight; it was buried under a pile of books. Thereafter, I sat down, straightened my body and wore a solemn look.

The visitor had to climb to the second floor, and the stairs were quite far from the gate. Even so, it was getting a bit too late. Impatient at the hold-up, as I walked towards the stairs, I saw my childhood friend Sukul coming up. The sight saddened me, even though we were meeting after years. I held him by his hand and sat him down on my bed, a phoney smile dancing on my lips.

'Missus is here too,' announced Sukul, making himself comfortable on the bed.

The news was like the first drizzle of Ashadh on my parched soul. I was happy. 'She is all by herself, doesn't even know her way up here, and yet, you've deserted her. You people know nothing of chivalry. Wait here, while I go fetch her.'

'Don't worry. She'll find her way up. Missus is a graduate. She must be buying copies of *Matwala*, impressed as she is with your writings,' Sukul said smilingly.

How could I have walked off after the revelation? I reined in my swollen pride and stayed firmly seated. A poet's imagination is never too off the mark, I told myself. After all, don't they say, 'Where the sun ceaseth, the poet reacheth'? Following a brief, solemn pause, I asked, 'Her Hindi must be excellent?'

'Yes,' replied Sukul, his voice oozing pride. 'She is a graduate.'

I felt a surge of reverence for Sukul's wife; these graduate ladies will truly emancipate our country, I told myself. Even though I was impatient for her darshan, I remain seated out of civility, variously picturing her sketchy image in my head. But once I returned to my senses, I thanked Sukul in my mind.

2

Sukul needs a proper introduction. He happens to be my schoolmate. Back in the day, he belonged to the tribe of boys who were ready to lose their heads but never their *choti*—the tuft of hair that epitomized their exalted caste. I could never quite understand how one could compare a man's honour with something as limp as a choti. I was of the opinion that an animal lives on even if its tail is cut off, but the severed tail withers and rots away. Moreover, a tail has skin, blood, bone and muscles. A choti, by contrast, is merely a clump of hair. It is lifeless, soulless.

On several occasions, I'd heard from the likes of Sukul—the fanatics of the cult of the choti—profound spiritual discourses on its significance. Yet, not once did I see the electricity of wisdom spark through the bulbous tuft nor grasped its essence. As a result, Sukul and I drifted apart into rival groups. His gang had Hindu boys who imagined themselves to be defenders of that faith, whereas mine comprised those who believed friendship was above religion. Naturally, in my group, all were welcome— Hindus, Muslims, farmers, everyone. We even had different playgrounds.

At times, following serious deliberations with my own group, I would visit Sukul's playground and watch him play hockey—with a sense of joy, wonder and deep appreciation, wide-eyed at his exploits. Meanwhile, the chotis atop each of Sukul's teammates—dangling like playing sticks, dancing to the rhythm of their nimble feet—were engaged in their own hockey match. Wali Mohammad often jested that when those blokes pirouetted on the playground, their tufts played tabla on their skulls. While Phillip quipped, 'See, the Hunter of the East has got the Hindu's forehead in a noose of hair.'

With time, Sukul's tuft and educational attainments, both grew dense. If there was ever a quarrel, he simply unknotted his choti, held the tuft aloft and proclaimed threateningly, 'I am a descendant of Chanakya.'

When the entrance exams drew near, Sukul's eyes were always bloodshot. A boy told me that he studied very diligently. At nights, he knotted his choti to a string, which in turn was tied to a peg hammered into the wall. The mechanism ensured that if he ever dozed off, he would be jolted back into wakefulness. Finally, I could see at least one earthly use of that choti.

By this time, I had earned a reputation as a poet, and, consequently, I saw no use of study. I spent my time marvelling at the mysteries of nature. At times, I would even counsel the boys that those who grovel to pass ordinary school exams, particularly when a book as profound as that of nature lay open before them—they were no better than weeds. On such occasions, the boys would look at me stunned, awed by my wisdom.

However, the adulation I enjoyed was short-lived. With less than ten days to the entrance exams, I suddenly lost my courage. As I contemplated my certain failure, poetry disappeared from nature; the beauties of the world were disfigured; my father's sacred form appeared terrifying, ghostly; instead of drizzling gently, my mother's love thundered incessantly. To preserve my clan's honour, I had been married off as a child. My young bride's singular beauty—once endlessly enchanting—now overflowed with the hemlock of hatred that spilled out of her enraged eyes. The townsfolk, who had once showered me with boundless affection, now began searing my soul with their contempt. And in the middle of all this, one day, I beheld the happy glow of diligence on Sukul's sunken face.

While books frightened me, the thought of putting them away added to my terror of failure. In effect, my imagination ran amuck: from deep space to the netherworlds. In fact, my imagination has never soared so high as it did back in the day. Perhaps, it has never since found such potent masala to propel its flight.

After much thought, I decided that I would teeter up to the door of the exam's imposing mansion, but, like a well-mannered boy, retreat without knocking too hard or pushing it violently open. In other words, I jumped the bandwagon. Since others had invested all their energies in the exams, they spent the pre-result phase calculating their possible scores. I, however, was clear-headed and, therefore, without a worry. I had adorned the dreary answer script for mathematics with the poet Padmakar's chirpy poems. Consequently, while others returned empty-handed from the examination hall, I managed to collect handfuls of lies, which I used judiciously to hoodwink others—father, mother, wife, relatives, townsfolk, everyone—as the situation demanded.

Everyone was rattled by my claim, made in an unflinching tone, that should the evaluations be honest, I would secure the first position in the entire district. My father was so taken in by the lie that his bearing became insolent. But as the day of results inched closer, my soul's lush creepers began to shrivel. I had left no scope for father's forgiveness, not even for a year's provisional pardon. Under the circumstances, running away from home seemed the only way out.

One day, I told my mother, 'The zamindars of Jagatpur have urged me to join a baraat—so earnestly as though

the wedding party would lose its sparkle without me.'
My mother was clearly moved by the announcement; an
invitation from the affluent zamindars was quite flattering.
She broke the news to my father: 'Have you heard this?
Your worthy child is now socializing with the zamindars.
They've invited him to join their wedding procession.'

'Then he must go. Buy him some clothing of his
choice and give him a little money for the expenses too,'
answered my father, suppressing his pride. Later, finding
me alone, my wife was prompt with her plea, 'Don't get so
dazzled by the nautch girls that I fade out of your memory.'

To allay her fears, I quoted a line from Kalidasa's
Raghuvansham. It means the following: 'How could a
mind, possessing such little knowledge, describe a glorious
clan, born of the sun?'

On hearing the words, she took a confident step towards
me, certain that I had praised her over the nautch girl, and
asked, 'Shouldn't I be told its meaning too?'

'Your body is delicate like a tender bamboo shoot, hers
is fat. Yours radiates sunlight, hers is all venom,' I explained
that Sanskrit quote to her, careful with the 'meaning'.

'Ah, stop it,' she blushed and returned to her chores,
her gait exuding pride and contentment.

My clothes were ready on time, and I was given the
promised money too. On the designated day, I set out for
the zamindars' baraat. However, shortly before reaching
the destination, I switched to a different road and reached
the railway station instead—just in time for the incoming
train. Thereafter, I bought a ticket to my in-laws' place and
wore a mourner's face throughout the journey.

My in-laws were alarmed to find me in that state. People flocked to me with anxious questions. 'There's been a bitter land dispute in the village. The matter has gone to the police. Since many of our enemies are injured in the skirmish, Father has been jailed. At the time of his arrest, he asked me to go to my father-in-law, collect three hundred rupees, the remainder of the dowry, return to the district the very next day and bail him out with the money,' I explained in a tone of dejection.

My father-in-law was struck dumb by the news, and my mother-in-law broke down. Father-in-law didn't have the money demanded of him. But my mother-in-law feared that if they weren't forthcoming with help, then, upon his release, Tripathiji would marry his son off to another girl. Mortified at the thought, she pawned off some of her jewellery for Rs 150—nose ring, bangles, anklets and such. 'Child, we couldn't raise more. As it is, we're always indebted to you. But we'll gradually pay the remaining amount too. With folded hands, I urge Tripathiji to have mercy on us,' pleaded my mother-in-law, handing over the money to me.

I assured her that I would never come to their home demanding the rest; it was indeed a grave crisis, but we would make do with whatever she could give. My kindness moved my father-in-law to tears. I bowed to him in deep reverence, touched his feet and returned to the station in a timely manner, to buy a ticket to Calcutta.

Hereafter, the foundation for my new life was laid. I learnt from the newspapers that Sukul had passed the exams in the first division. Four years later, he got a BA degree, followed by an MA degree. I kept track of his progress. Eventually, he found a good job too. Having passed all the exams, he became an examiner himself. By contrast, my own life remained largely unchanged. I erred once and kept erring thereafter; having failed that first exam, I failed in all the other exams too. I appeared for one exam after another, but to no avail.

Today, I met Sukul for the first time since those days. His visit brought the past vividly to life in my mind. All these years later, everything stands changed. My parents are gone, my wife is dead. Only I remain, clung to my same old self. Surrounded by a dreary field of daily exams, swept over by countless waves of questions.

3

For a while, I was lost in thoughts. When I returned to my senses, I saw the very embodiment of beauty standing in front of me, staring at me with unwavering eyes. She joined her palms in a namaskar and greeted me in elegant English. 'Good morning, poet of verse libre,' she said. I sprang to my feet, returned her namaskar and courteously invited her to sit, my stretched hand pointing to the chair next to Sukul's.

At my behest, she walked to the chair, her steps slow, her body swaying gently. Once seated, she turned to me and said smilingly, 'You write really well.'

A parched deer fails to see the truth about a mirage—the fact that it is not a soothing lake but a cruel joke. This was the first time such fulsome praise was lavished on me. I had a fleeting desire to run to Mahesh Babu, drag him to the scene and proudly announce that the fountain of nectar had finally burst forth. He, too, should cup his palms and collect a little of it. However, given the amount of nectar that had sprung, I wasn't satisfied myself; I was keen for more. Hence I sat quietly, observing the lady with the reverence of a lonely devotee.

'Sukul can't understand your poems, but I explain them to him,' she said, sending yet more nectar flowing through her crimson lips. At this, Sukul couldn't restrain himself and said, 'Truth be told, I've never come across anyone explaining poetry so well. And what can I say of the impact it produces? Even if you don't get a word of it, you're never bored. I can't think of a single professor—not even in my MA classes—whose lectures packed a greater punch.'

'Oh, yes, sir,' exclaimed the lady, straightening her spine. 'A study of this variety extends beyond your MA classes. But when you passed your MA, you wore a cubit-long choti. And your intelligence, like your choti, was lifeless and stiff. Like a nail stuck into a wall.'

I knew Sukul's choti better than I ever knew him. However, upon his arrival, it had somehow gone unnoticed. But just as I raised my eyes to inquire after its well-being, the lady intercepted me. 'You're radiant like the moon. I wish you'd done something for your friend, too, and turned Sukul into a *su-kul*, a man of an illustrious lineage. You have to trust me—trying to sharpen his intellect is really exhausting.'

I was summoning the courage to speak up and thank her. But then she added, 'I am not Sukul's consort.'

At this, I went pale with shock. However, she looked fixedly at me and went on, as though teasing me, 'But he is my consort.' Now I looked thoroughly puzzled, as writers are known to be. Once again, she cast her kind glance on me and said, 'I wish you could be my consort too.'

I was shocked. 'Is her idea of marriage the same as Draupadi's?' I asked myself.

Just then the lady looked at her wristwatch and stood up. 'It's getting late. Let us leave. I have come to fetch you. The taxi is waiting,' she said, her brows arched. Thereafter, she approached me, rested her palm on my shoulder and asked in a honeyed voice, 'You do eat chicken, don't you?'

I looked at Sukul questioningly. But he offered only a smile. I took a moment to process her question and replied, 'I do, for long, as a matter of principle.'

And then she set off. I followed Sukul out, my shawl draped clumsily around me.

4

Throughout the journey, a barrage of thoughts wrestled in my head. No, our society doesn't extend such liberty, certainly not to a woman. There is no way one could be free to eat chicken. I do so but only stealthily. Could this lady . . .? And Sukul is, after all, a Sukul—an extremely orthodox Brahmin.

We reached Sukul's residence, a modest two-storey house in a colony of Bengalis. The locality was littered with heaps of garbage, with stinking scales of fish piled on top.

We got off the car and headed inside. To the left of the entrance was a small sitting room, where a maid was playing with a child of one and a half years. Upon seeing the lady, the baby got impatient and started crying, 'Ma, Ma!' It then jumped into the maid's lap, dangled itself out and reached for the mother, its arm outstretched. The lady was pleased at the sight.

'Isn't the child yours?' I asked.

She laughed and said, 'Mine? What makes you doubt it? But I don't produce milk.'

I thought to myself—she is educated, young but perhaps yet to experience the pangs of motherhood. That is why she doesn't lactate. I thanked the Creator.

'Come, let us go upstairs. We'll talk alone while Sukul goes out to the market to buy chicken,' she said, returning the child to the maid.

I followed her, wondering wildly if a romantic possibility lurked in the solitude upstairs. I had difficulty stemming in my emotions; my heart throbbed with joyous anticipation.

It was a tastefully appointed bedroom. 'Please sit,' she said and turned away to light the stove. And I sat dumbstruck, marvelling at her reflection in the mirror as she primed the stove.

5

She laid out tea, paan and cigarettes on the table, and then sat herself down. 'Please help yourself,' she urged sweetly, holding out a cup of tea for me. I accepted it politely, clutching the farther edge of the saucer, my eyes conveying gratitude.

She brought her cup to her lips, a gentle smile lighting up her face, her gaze lowered. Once the cup was half empty, she turned to me and asked, 'You are a person of my own faith—aren't you?'

Her question triggered a surge of waves, deep in my stomach, and in the teacup too. I could feel the lashing tempest. Such was the force of her question that many a grand mansion of emotions, built along the dark cloudy beach of the mind, were completely blown away. 'But aren't you Sukul's . . .' I muttered.

'Wife? Yes, that I am.'

'Then how do I . . .?'

'Make you my wife?' she completed my question.

I had never faced such a conundrum in my life. My deep sea of emotions vapourized instantly. The tempest that had raged at it was gone—to a shore unknown. Only a lifeless desert was left behind, which, under the circumstances, scorched me all the more pitilessly.

Seeing me grow so withdrawn and lost, she intervened. 'I'm sorry to be so blunt, but I have noticed men suffer from an innate idiocy, which comes to the fore particularly when they interact with a woman.'

My safety lay in meekly submitting to her views. 'Right you are. In front of a woman, a man's intelligence has no use.'

'Indeed,' she added. 'I've completely failed trying to make a man out of Sukul. Take, for example, the word "bibi". I can be Sukul's bibi—which, by the way, I am—but I can be yours too.'

The possibility rained a little joy on my desert of a heart. Without giving it much thought, I blurted out, 'Yes, of course.'

'You still don't get it. So what if you're a litterateur? You are, after all, Sukul's friend. You see, bibi is an expansive term,' she said, her tone betraying her sense of exasperation.

'Definitely,' I added.

But she went on, paying no attention to me. 'Younger sister, niece, daughter, younger brother's wife —the word "bibi" can be used for all of them. What did you mean when you said "yes"?'

It felt as if I finally saw the depths of the water I was swimming in, having drowned and downed a few mouthfuls. 'In the sense of a younger sister,' I answered, trying hard to appear pleased with the conversation.

'Ah, you see? To be a man is to uphold one's words.'

'Indeed, call me not a man if I retract my statement,' I uttered the words with added emphasis, for my reputation was at stake.

She blushed at my rejoinder. For a moment, she avoided looking me in the eye. But then she composed herself and came to the point, stating her position plainly. 'We are in great distress. For a year now, we've been running around for cover. I've been asking Sukul about all his friends, trying to identify those who can help us. But only your description appeared reassuring. However, we didn't have your address. We have been looking for you for over a year.'

I looked at her eyes; they were brimming with tears. 'I'm ready,' I declared.

She sprang to her feet, walked up to me and held my hands. 'Brother, please protect me. Sukul has been cut off from his family. Please accept me into your clan, so that I may be duly wedded to Sukul.'

A few drops rolled down her big, beautiful eyes and dripped on to my thighs. I too stood up, wiped her tears with the end of my *chadar* and proclaimed, 'Hereafter, you're my uncle's daughter, my younger sister. My uncle came to

Bengal with his wife and lived out his days there. He had a daughter, too, who was born in the ancestral village. You are that daughter and this shall be your story.'

Filled with joy, she clasped my hands gratefully. Just then, Sukul too walked back from the market. 'So, has the epic been narrated?' he said.

'Not yet. Just the prelude before the complete saga unfolds,' I replied.

'Sukul, Columbus has finally spotted the coast,' she added, choking up with emotions.

Sukul approached me with happy steps and asked, 'Is there some tea left?'

'All of it. But it may have gone cold. Get it warmed.' I then turned to Bibi and asked, 'But I couldn't gather your name yet.'

'At the place I've come from, I am known as Pukhraj. Over here, I'm Pushpkumari.'

'Kunwar, hurry up. Your chicken recipe may be tasty, but your story is tastier. I'm eager for both.'

Kunwar busied herself preparing tea. As she pumped at the stove, her *aanchal* slipped off her head. But she didn't bother drawing it up again. Sukul's eyes, like hungry bumblebees, were feasting on her face.

6

I took a bath, draped Sukul's dhoti around my waist and ate a wholesome Muslim meal; bread, curry, chutney, murabba and sweets, everything was prepared in an unmistakable Muslim style of cooking. While eating, I asked, 'Kunwar, are you any good at cooking Hindu food?'

'Yes,' she said and looked at Sukul, indicating that she had learnt it from Sukul.

'Ditching your books for the kitchen—must have been a big decision for you,' I remarked.

'I can put up with everything for Sukul,' she answered resolutely.

The meal was over. We went back to the same room. Sukul carried the child too. Chewing betel leaves, I said, 'Do not delay any longer, Kunwar.'

Kunwar went downstairs briefly, passed on a few instructions to the maid, shut the door leading to the upper floor and returned to her chair.

'It should be *shubhashya sheeghram*—the sooner, the better,' I reiterated.

Kunwar said, 'My mother is a Hindu. She belongs to the Vajpayee family of Lucknow. I am from that clan.'

'Then you are of a noble lineage,' I said. 'What is your father's name?'

'Why take his name?' Kunwar said. 'Don't you remember? Your uncle is my father.'

It was a painful question; Kunwar choked up. She paused to compose herself and said, 'Vajpayeeji was not content with one marriage. So he married again. I was in my mother's womb at the time. We were at my maternal grandmother's place in Bihita. My nani, our lone support, was the last one left of the family. But she, too, passed away. Such is God's will. My mother wrote several letters to her father-in-law, but he ignored them. When she could no longer eke out a living, my mother sold off all the utensils and used the money to travel to Lucknow. But the moment she set foot in the house, both her husband and her father-in-law turned brutally hostile. The husband alleged: "The child is your sin, not ours." Her father-in-law thundered: "She's a woman of loose morals. She has come all this way to corrupt our dharma. Had she been virtuous, she wouldn't have dragged herself here. Her people there would have raised the child." The neighbours, too, joined in with their opinions, and the co-wife raised a shindy. One cruel night, her husband grabbed her by the arms and kicked her out of the house. With no roof over her head, my mother drifted about on the dark streets.

'The next morning, a man took pity on her. He was a Muslim. You can easily imagine the amount of reverence she must have had for the Hindu faith, dharma and the Gods in that hour of distress. That helpless, broken woman sought nothing but a refuge—one that promised compassion and humanity. She found that in a Muslim. He wasn't a lecherous man. His manners were upright. He was reassuring, trustworthy and chivalrous—qualities any woman seeks in a man. Naturally, Mother felt drawn to him. He took her along. He led the way, Mother followed.

'As she walked behind the Muslim man, dressed in sari and wearing *phool* bangles, her Hindu identity became all the more conspicuous. A follower of Arya Samaj spotted this odd pair and was promptly hot on the trail. The Muslim man hurried home. He was frightened, as he could sense he was being tailed by a Hindu. The Aryasamaji identified his house and went away to inform the police. Meanwhile, the Muslim man, too, set his precautionary plans in motion. He put my mother in a Muslim friend's curtained tonga and got her smuggled away to another Muslim friend's residence.

'Following the Aryasamaji's complaint, the police launched an investigation, while my mother hopped from one Muslim house to another. Finally, she ended up at a house that belonged to a police inspector. At that time he was on leave. Later, when he returned to his place of work, he took my mother along. He was single and my mother was beautiful.'

I wanted to know the name of the Inspector Sahab, but then I thought I should find that out later, along with Vajpayeeji's first name.

Kunwar continued, 'This was how Inspector Sahab came to the rescue of a helpless woman. Sometime later, I was born. Over the years, I had quite a few brothers and sisters. Initially, I used to study only Urdu. But when my Muslim father was transferred to Lucknow, I started learning English.

'I was in the ninth grade when I first overheard my parents discussing my marriage. I was standing outside the room, unbeknownst to them. That day, I got a whiff of things. I learnt the truth about the slanderous adjectives he would often hurl at my mother in anger. It opened my eyes to the reality; I felt ashamed of having taken sides in the Hindu–Muslim dispute. One day, I cornered my mother and, having told her all that I'd heard and understood, pleaded to her that she explain the rest of it. When we were alone, my mother shared the story of her ordeal, described it as God's will and then fell silent.

'I was disgusted with the notion of caste pride. I declared, "I will not get married. I want to study to my heart's content." That was when my ideas changed. After passing the matriculation exam, I joined the IT College and took up Hindi along with other subjects. Having passed my FA exam, I moved to BA. It was here that I found Sukul, in my last year of college.'

The second 'I found Sukul' was uttered, Kunwar burst forth crying. I savoured the tender moments and then said, 'Kunwar, take your time and describe it well. Hindi storytellers and readers are eager for such accounts too.'

Kunwar straightened her back, took a firm position and resumed her story. 'Back then, Sukul was a professor at Christian College. He had assured his principal that he considered Christianity to be the greatest religion in the world. And that it was only out of respect for his elderly father—who may not live beyond three–four years—that he had delayed formal conversion. He even wrote a few essays to announce his belief. Convinced, the visionary principal recommended his candidature, and he got the position.

'He rented a house right across mine. He would take great care to adjust his hat, lest his choti became visible. It was like Vibhishan hiding his *tilak* beneath his turban, so his allegiance to Ram stayed a secret. Sometimes, Mrs Sukul visited him, but mostly, he lived alone. He knew me to the extent that I was a college girl and lived in a neighbouring house.

'One evening, I was on my terrace. Sukul was sitting on the veranda. The weather was rainy. The clouds had arranged themselves as the garland of Kamadeva, the god of love. A cool breeze blew all around. Trees and plants were swaying wildly. What can I say? The weather had me enchanted, and I, too, swayed with the wind.

'Long ago, I had stacked some bricks to climb on and gaze beyond the terrace parapet. That evening, I stepped on them again. As I looked over the edge of the parapet, my eyes fell on Sukul. He was just sitting there. I had seen him earlier too, but he hadn't noticed me ever. This time, our eyes met. He sported an army officer's moustache, and his face was as fearsome as that of a tiger, but his eyes were dreamy like Kalidasa's. Forgive my impertinence—I use the name Kalidasa for billy goats.

'I was smitten by the sight. A ticklish sensation coursed through my body. The experience was so electrifying that I couldn't control my emotions and at once delivered a military salute to Sukul. But upon returning to my senses, I blushed and slumped to the floor. Thereafter, for several days, our eyes didn't meet, even though I stole many a secret glance at him.

'Sukul, too, seemed restless. He kept looking out for me, carefully evading others' gazes. I started enjoying this game. I felt the thrill of a hunter when the prey appears nervy. Sukul began camping on the veranda all day long. He would look around to rule out any prying eyes and then direct his gaze at my terrace. The empty terrace caused him to heave sighs of sadness, while I followed his desperate antics through a hole in the parapet.

'One day, I felt the desire to ingratiate him with a darshan. I was in the habit of scattering the bricks after each furtive rendezvous. I collected them again and mounted the stack. The sun had risen right in front of him. The moment Sukul saw me, he joined his hands in a pranam. I was carrying a piece of paper. I rolled it into a ball and threw it down. Sukul eyed it greedily, more greedily than Nadir Shah had eyed the Kohinoor or the British had eyed Awadh.'

'What was scribbled in it?' I asked, unable to contain my excitement.

'Nothing—it was brightly transparent, like the Kohinoor. Sukul picked it up in one fell swoop and unrolled it fondly. Had I written him a note, perhaps he wouldn't have relished it as much. But the blank sheet recited to him all the poems the lovelorn souls of this world had ever written. He carried it to the veranda and pressed it against his heart, making sure I noticed that gesture. I smiled and took his leave.

'Thereafter, I stopped firing blank shots. The cannons I now fired had verses from Bihari, Dev, Padmakar, Matiram and such. Not too long afterwards, Sukul's castle began caving in. One day, I fired a cannon with a specific instruction: "I'll visit your home. Leave the doors open all night long." And I did visit him. Having invaded and proclaimed my ownership of the fortress, I made it clear to him that after the exams I would move in for good. Sukul panicked, calling our love an error of judgement: "What were we thinking? What have we come to?"

'I surely hadn't erred. But yes, in marrying him off to Mrs Sukul, perhaps his father had made a terrible mistake. I did, however, consider the fact that through my actions, I may have added to Sukul's woes. But come to think of it, aren't we all hounded by troubles on all sides? Now that it was resolved, there was no going back.

'While Sukul persisted with his missteps, I aced it right for the start. I sat for my exams, passed with flying colours and also earned the Raibahadur Bammulal Medal for distinction in Hindi. It was in Sukul's house that I learnt of my results. However, I never went back to the college to collect my degree.

'When I first ran off to Sukul's house, right after my exams, there was a massive uproar. Unable to trace me, people concluded I had taken off with someone. Sukul was a natural suspect. Following the failed search, a police complaint was filed. Sukul was deeply unnerved by the events—he couldn't decide where to hide me. Sukul's house had a brick closet built right into the wall. There was a small vault below it. You see how thin I am now? Back then, I was even skinnier.

'A few months ago, at Lord Jagannath's temple, I saw a statue of Kaliyuga—it was the figure of a man rebuking his old father, even as he carried his wife aloft his shoulders and held his little boy by his finger. How I wished for Sukul to become Kaliyuga. On many occasions, I did taste a little success in transforming him. I would tell him to imagine his father embodying debauched Hindu orthodoxies and goad him to rebuke that form of his. And rebuke he did!

'Considering my size, the vault was big enough for me to slip into it. Whenever I went in hiding, I would tell Sukul to heap some clothes on top of me and not to worry. I would always manage to breathe through an opening. The upper shelves of the closet were anyway packed with odds and ends. Once everything was set, I'd ask Sukul to put a lock on the closet. I practiced staying in that position for long hours, sometimes two hours at a stretch, sometimes three.

'Whenever Sukul left for college, he would lock the door. And upon his return, he kept it bolted from inside.

If someone came knocking, I would quickly disappear into the vault, and the closet would be locked. Only then would Sukul answer the knock.

'It was on the third day that the police party arrived at our doorstep. After taking the usual precautionary measures, Sukul opened the door. It was morning—no, rather it was dawn. The inspector was a Muslim, rigorous with his duties. He approached the closet and stood next to it. I could make out that he was trying to catch the sound of breathing, so I started breathing through my mouth. A few tense moments followed. Luckily, the closet was left alone, and after rummaging through a few drawers, the inspector closed the search. Sukul saw him off, bolted the door and returned to pull me out. Set free, I laughed out loud and then advised Sukul to quickly take another house on rent.

'Before long, the news of the police search spread everywhere. It reached Sukul's village too. Sukul himself wrote a letter home, telling them all about the raid, but not before he had moved to a new house. It was a big one, with two courtyards. It was chosen keeping my needs in view. Upon receiving the letter, Sukul's brother promptly arrived with Mrs Sukul, to take stock of the situation. We were already prepared for the eventuality. Sukul and his wife settled in the bigger half of the house, while I continued to live my secret life across the other courtyard.

'I had no troubles in life, but Sukul's duties grew twofold. Mrs Sukul stayed here for three–four months, but after a sudden, rather unfortunate week-long bout of fever, she passed away. By then, his brother had already left for the village. Sukul didn't call anyone from his family and performed her final rites alone, with the help of a few local friends.

'By then I had already learnt all about you from Sukul. I knew that I had to take charge of my own ship, but I couldn't find your whereabouts. That worry persisted. When Mrs Sukul was still around, I'd even sent Mr Sukul looking for you in your village. I had no doubt that only someone like you could become my support. You see, I faced no obstacles even when Mrs Sukul was alive. But now that she's gone, life hasn't become any easier. Late Mrs Sukul is the mother of this child.

'With the passing of Mrs Sukul, we were left with no choice but to change our identity and disappear. We had enough savings to cover more than a year's expenses. Thankfully, after many days of looking around, our efforts bore fruit: we found your address.'

I thanked Kunwar for the food and, before taking leave of her, assured her that I would make all the necessary arrangements for her wedding in Calcutta itself.

7

Sethji was sitting idly. Taking him to a secluded place, I explained all about the situation. He agreed to the idea. 'But don't tell Munshiji. He can never keep a secret,' he cautioned.

Once the position of the celestial bodies was found to be auspicious, the wedding preparations were set in motion. And then, on an auspicious day, in the presence of Hindi-speaking writers who had assembled from various parts of the country, the marriage of Sukul and Pushpkumari was solemnized.

Many Kanojia Brahmins partook of the wedding feast. And even before the newlyweds could set foot in Sukul's village, the good news of their marriage had reached the place. Kunwar is still alive.

Jyotirmayee[*]

1

'And so we must meekly obey? Because people like you and the hostile scriptures you've authored have kept us enslaved? Because there seems to be no way out? Is this fair?' asked the seventeen-year-old moon-faced beauty. Her eyes, large as the petals of a lotus, shone brightly.

'But a faithful wife, after leading a life of austerity and penance, reunites with her husband in heaven,' answered the young man, his tone tranquil. He was now staring at the girl, with the probing eyes of an inquisitor.

At this, the girl smiled, and a crimson hue washed over her face. Her lips, red like a bed of roses in full bloom, parted gently, releasing a radiant, playful glee on her mystery-cloaked visage. And then, they were shut again.

'What a pathetic utterance!' decried the girl in Sanskrit. 'Pray tell me: if the first wife, after her death, awaits her

---

[*] Published in 1949 in a collection of stories titled *Lili*.

venerable husband in heaven, and the husband sends more dead wives heavenwards—the second, the third, the fourth—demanding that each awaits his arrival, which of the four would he eventually unite with upon his own death?' Having posed that riddle, she burst into laughter. The young man's face turned pale with an air of offended dignity.

'You've completed your MA this year. That, too, in English. Perhaps you've spent more time reading biographies of faithful women than histories of faithful husbands,' added the lady, sharpening her barbs.

The young man was visiting his brother's in-laws, and the combative girl was his brother's sister–in–law, a widow.

'What sort of education have you received?' the young man asked, a note of derision apparent in his tone.

'Only Hindi and a smattering of Sanskrit,' answered the girl as she collected the betel box to prepare a fold of paan.

'Well, all I can say is that your ideas might set our society—already combustible as a dried-out straw—violently aflame,' observed the young man, casting looks of amazement at the girl.

'But society is also keen on melting my heart away—already fragile as a wax doll. It is that raging fire which threatens to tear my heart asunder. Pray, do mention this truth too,' countered the girl. 'Back then, I was all of twelve. I had never been to my *sasural*, not even known my husband. Yet, I became a widow,' she added, her large eyes inflamed, her fingers dipped in the lime bowl. As she completed the sentence, a few drops of tears trickled on to her thighs. But she restrained herself, wiped her eyes dry with her *aanchal* and resumed rolling the paan.

'Do you like tobacco?' asked the girl.

'No.' A dead silence echoed through his soul. He had never heard a young widow make such daring and dangerous observations. He believed that these matters never spilled out of the newspapers into the real world; to him, it was merely a newspaper-fuelled revolution. But he could not fathom how a young woman like her, born in the exalted clan of the Kanyakubj Brahmins, could share those sentiments. He was visibly unsettled by her views.

'Here, take it,' said the girl, holding out the fold of paan.

'Please don't let my words offend you. I was just trying to test the limits of your compassion,' observed the girl, her tone cold.

Although the young man took the paan from her, he showed no intention of chewing on it.

'Please do savour it,' urged the young girl and added, 'May I ask you something?'

'Sure, go ahead,' answered the young man.

'What if someone asks you to marry a widow?' she asked, a mischievous smile playing on her lips.

'What answer can I give to a question like that? It's for my father to decide whom I should marry,' he explained bashfully.

'But what if you were your own master?' she pressed forth.

Although he was hesitant, he mustered a little courage and answered, 'I am not comfortable with the idea of widow remarriage.'

She was visibly affected by the answer; tears welled up in her eyes. But she composed herself, cast a quick glance at the man and then lowered her gaze.

The young man was to return the next day. He said his goodbyes, received blessings from the elderly women of the house, but his eyes kept seeking that young girl. Except that she was nowhere to be seen. At last, he climbed down to the ground floor, only to find her waiting by the door.

'I'll take your permission now. I'm leaving for my home.'

The girl offered her salutations with folded hands and handed him a letter. 'Please visit us again soon.'

Upon receiving the letter, a strange sensation of happiness thrilled his heart. He felt drawn to her eyes. Like a celestial nymph, those eyes were eager to soar to the sky, flapping their wing-like blue eyelids; fly away to the world of love's eternal spring, where the reigning deities of love—Madan and Rati—are known to meet and frolic, where no manner of cruel custom could compel the new-fangled to yield, where eyes sparkle with love's endearing images, throats pour fourth sweet melodies, the heart is home to the truest of feelings and man's form is aglow with beauty.

'Jyoti . . .' the young man uttered her name, his voice sweet, his tone caring.

Emboldened by the utterance, Jyotirmayee advanced towards the young man with uninhibited steps, until she was very close. Her head all but touching his chin, their eyes locked. That gentle brush of clothes set off a strange current running through the pores of their bodies, the like of which neither had known nor experienced. Their stirred bodies oozed atoms of exhilaration, their eyes were drunk with joy.

'I'll say it some other time.' And the young man set off, somewhat embarrassed.

'Please, do remember. With folded hands, I urge you to . . .' But the young man had disappeared.

2

'Viren, that letter can move even the most stonehearted,' observed Vijay, as if pitying Jyotirmayee.

'But are you so faint-hearted? Can't you rescue a single life that the cruel customs of our society are sure to crush? What good is your education? To turn you into a tamed bull, harnessed to carts plying along the same old roads?' Virendra railed at his friend.

'I have no power over my father, Viren. I can't defy his wishes. But trust me, I'll live my days with the regret that I couldn't save an innocent flower adrift in the river of this merciless society. That, too, because the same society never taught me how to swim against its own harsh currents.'

'But now you've also earned wisdom of a different sort, which has given you the skills to swim.'

'Yes, it has, but only the talent to paddle along the stream. Not the daring to swim across to the steps of its ghat. The way I see it, all the ghats have been usurped by society. And it is impossible for any human being to swim forever.'

'But if not to the clean concrete ghats, you can always reach for the muddy riverbank.'

'But not with that pristine flower, not so long as I'm prohibited from taking her to any of the ghats. The riverbank is so swampy and overgrown that my tired legs will never find a firm footing. Besides, there is the blazing social gaze that will not only cause the flower to wither but singe me as well.'

'In conclusion, you lack the guts to rescue that sinless, defenceless girl from the muck in which society has mired her. The one who's showered you with all her love, shared her secret fears with you, thinking you were her soulmate.'

'Look here, she has indeed stolen my heart. But as for my body—it belongs to my father, Viren. And in this matter, I'm quite helpless myself.'

'What rubbish! This is the greatest self-deception, Vijay. Can the heart be torn asunder from the body? The one who conquers your heart so effortlessly also wins over your body. To humiliate her now is to humiliate yourself. Is she exempted from obeying social laws? Won't society cast her out, too, as one discards broken pots and pans? Has she not mulled over the consequences herself?'

'I'm certain her feelings are corrupted with those "other" desires too.'

'Had she been so gripped by those "other" desires, by now she would've fled the home your brother is married into, smearing their fair upper-caste faces with the black ink of ignominy. Don't you get it? She is a wise girl. It wasn't lust that made her bare her heart to you. She truly loves you. Now tell me, what's her address?'

Virendra pulled out his notebook, scribbled her address and said, 'You're my friend, she's my friend's beloved.' The two exchanged knowing glances and started laughing.

3

Many months had passed since that incident. Yet, the mere thought of visiting his brother's sasural sent shivers down his spine; cold hesitation froze his limbs. He was a prisoner of his own pledge.

Noticing his friend sink into such a miserable state, Virendra felt deep remorse. Since that episode, he made certain not to inflict any more of his wishes on Vijay. Vijay was now a research scholar at Allahabad University, whereas Virendra, having completed his BA, was managing his family business. He was the only son of Mansaram Aggarwal, the famous magnate from Itawa who owned the Nagarmal–Bikhamdas firm.

It had been nearly a month since Virendra had returned to Itawa. Before leaving, he did say his farewell to Vijay. Vijay too was set to return home. Three–four days ago, a letter had arrived, summoning him to his birthplace—district Unnaon, village Beeghapur.

Vijay's father was reasonably well-off. He was a Mishra from Majhgaon, a high-born Kanyakubj. In the hope of receiving a large dowry, Mishraji had stalled Vijay's wedding; so far, none of the families had promised more than Rs 3000. However, of late, he seemed a bit inclined towards a recent proposal. This family was based in Moradabad. Some fifteen days earlier, they had collected Vijay's horoscope for scrutiny. Since the stars seemed propitiously aligned, someone from the prospective bride's family had come to firm up everything again. Meanwhile, Vijay's uncle and father were busy debating the matter over.

'Dada, there is one problem, though—they are Sanadhya Brahmins, of the agrarian kind. What if we are socially boycotted?'

'You and your fears! My only concern is money. If we have money, all the bastards will come flocking to us—friends, kinsfolk, people of our caste, community, everyone. Otherwise none shall bother extending even the smallest of courtesies.'

'So what do you propose?'

'Go ahead with the wedding, what else?'

'But they refuse to budge beyond seven thousand rupees.'

'Don't you see? The bride's relative is camping doggedly at our home. Plunder him leisurely and take care the prey doesn't scamper away.'

'He's hopelessly trapped.'

'That he is. Besides, what's there to worry about? The baraat will comprise only four of us from the immediate family. We'll tell them it was too distant, and we didn't get enough dowry to cover the travel expenses.'

'And the money thus saved can be used to fund the wedding feast here. Correct?'

'Yes, that's correct.'

'Indeed, the only reasonable thing to do.'

Wearing wooden clogs, the duo—Vijay's father, Pandit Gangadhar Mishra, and uncle Pandit Krishnashankar—clattered back into the house and sat solemnly on a twine cot laid out in the *baithak*. They had bent their heads low, to look pensive; their foreheads were emblazoned with crimson sandal tilaks and their necks adorned with *rudraksh* beads.

The man representing the bride's party—the turbaned Pandit Satyanarayan Sharma—was dressed plainly in a rugged *mirzaee*. He was waiting nervously on a bamboo cot. Seeing Mishraji return, he asked submissively, 'What's your command for me?'

Pandit Gangadhar pointed at Pandit Krishnashankar and answered, 'Work out the final details with him. He heads this family.'

Following the cue, Pandit Satyanarayan turned towards Pandit Krishnashankar and looked at him reverentially. At this point, Pandit Krishnashankar spoke up. 'Panditji, the fact is this—the dowry you've offered is quite meagre. We've already spent seven to eight thousand on the boy's education. You must consider this too. Sometime back, the Vajpayees of Lucknow were here. Although they're already related to us, we had to decline their proposal. They were only offering six thousand. If the dowry doesn't even cover the basic wedding expenses, to what end did we educate our boy? If we don't profit out of this relationship,' he paused, cast furtive glances around and continued, 'why would we come down to your . . .?'

'I see. Please tell me whatever you wish for,' Pandit Satyanarayan said.

'Fifteen thousand,' blurted Pandit Krishnashankar.

'In that case, we'll have to sell off every last utensil at home,' Pandit Krishnashankar replied, alarmed at the figure.

'What's your final offer?'

'Please accept nine thousand.'

'Okay, let us settle for twelve.'

Rattled by the negotiation, Pandit Satyanarayan clutched at his seat.

'Would you agree to eleven?' asked Pandit Krishnashankar, a note of irritation apparent in his voice.

'Ten thousand is a fair amount,' Pandit Satyanarayan countered, sounding resolute.

'Okay, done. But we'll take five upfront, as advance.'

Pandit Satyanarayan pulled out a piece of paper, a legal stamp and five banknotes of a thousand each. 'Here, please sign this deed. But first write the following: As per the duly testified terms for the marriage of Pandit Satyanarayan's (Moradabad) daughter with Shri Vijay Kumar Mishra, MA, which is settled at ten thousand rupees, inclusive of *gauna* expenses, I have received an advance payment of five thousand rupees from the bride's father. Then sign across the stamp, mentioning your father's name too.'

Pandit Gangadhar was beside himself with joy. All the paperwork was quickly got through, and the date of the wedding was finalized.

Before long, the tilak ceremony, which involved ritual lavishing of gifts on the groom, was concluded. Until the tilak, Vijay would often think of Jyotirmayee. But the prospect of marriage soon occupied his thoughts. And by and by, as is usually the case, that diminishing memory sunk to the very bottom of his consciousness. In fact, at times he even doubted her moral character. 'What a real quagmire it was. A lucky escape for me,' he thought to himself. Sometimes he called to mind the Sanskrit maxim from the Manusmriti: 'If a woman's character, much as a man's fate, remains inscrutable even to the Gods, could mortals be any wiser?'

4

Vijay had written to Virendra, urging him to join the wedding celebrations. But Virendra declined the invitation saying, 'I am friends with Vijay, the victorious—not with *parajay*, the vanquished. I cannot bring myself to attend this wedding.'

As planned, Pandit Gangadhar, citing the great hurry, did not invite most of his relatives, except a select few. That was why the invitation never reached Jyotirmayee's family. But very few turned up even from the places where the invitation cards did reach. The air was thick with rumours and suspicion.

Before long, the baraat took off. In Lucknow, Vijay ran into Virendra. 'Yaar, you seem to have forgotten all about Jyotirmayee, so charmed are you with this wedding.'

'Truth be told: women like her serve no purpose in society.'

'Look at you. You're such a turncoat,' scoffed Virendra.

'What choice do I have?'

'Tell me something. Where is the proof that the girl you're marrying now is chaste beyond doubt, like Sati Savitri?'

'There is a difference between an unwed woman and a widow,' Vijay shot back.

'Yes, I believe so too.'

'One must do well to remember the importance of customs and culture. Only the cultured beget noble offspring.'

'Wow! You've become an accomplished astrologer too.'

'Is that so?'

'Indeed. Well, in that case,' added Virendra, 'I feel like coming along.'

'Come you must! Hadn't I sent a letter pleading your presence? But you have no care for the mundane realities of this world. You are too busy raising and razing walls of abstract ideas.'

'I get your point, brother. Let's get a taste of reality too. Tell me, how much did you profit?'

'Ten thousand.'

'Ten thousand! I'm sure you haven't spared even a single utensil of value at the bride's home.'

'They're Kanyakubj Brahmins, from an affluent family.'

'I suspect they come from a lower class of Brahmins.'

'No, not so low. Their worth is set at seventeen *biswa* land.*'

'Hmmm,' was all he said before losing himself in some thought. 'You disgust me,' declared Virendra, following a brief silence. 'No, now I won't go. You're such a lowly man,' he added and went off towards the city.

The baraat headed to Moradabad, as scheduled.

5

The marriage was solemnized. Pandit Satyanarayan played a wonderful host to the baraat, entertaining his guests with all his heart. When the rituals came to an end, he gifted a silver bowl loaded with Rs 5000 in cash. Another 5000, over and above the agreed dowry, was given away in kind— as a gift of jewellery to the bride. Vijay, too, was pampered with expensive presents. Among other things, he was given

---

* Biswa is a unit of land measurement. Here it denotes the land endowment a subgroup of Brahmins is traditionally entitled to. In this intra-caste hierarchy, 20 biswa is the upper limit, reserved only for the subgroup at the apex.

a gold chain, a pocket watch, a wristwatch, a bicycle and a gold ring. Each one with the baraat—young and old—had the cockles of their heart warmed.

On the fourth day after the wedding, the baraat returned with the bride. Pandit Satyanarayan had reserved a second-class compartment for the newlyweds, while an inter-class compartment was arranged for the rest. As the baraat was departing, Pandit Satyanarayan bid farewell to Pandit Gangadhar and Pandit Krishnashankar, his hands folded in a gesture of obeisance. He then turned to the bride and said, 'Child, send me a letter as soon as you reach.' And then the train trundled away.

By the time they reached Prayag, Vijay had grown restless with excitement. The time had come to behold the unseen face that had triggered countless fantasies. His heart overflowed with joy and gratitude; he thanked his father, father-in-law and the entire society. His desire to lift the veil of his young bride, his only co-passenger in the compartment, was as strong as a chakori bird's longing for the moon.* The train moved at its top speed.

Vijay could no longer stem in his urges. He rose from his seat and sat himself next to the bride, his body trembling with excited anticipation. As he lifted his hand to remove the *ghoonghat*, he could feel his wrist shaking too. Oh, what joy there was in trembling thus! Each hair on his body was stimulated with a gush of exhilaration.

---

* Chakori is a mythical bird, often likened to a partridge. Since the bird quenches its thirst only with raindrops that fall during the moon's transit to the Swati Nakshatra, it constantly longs for the moon.

Just as Vijay lifted the ghoonghat, he recoiled in shock and shrieked, 'My goodness! It's you?'

'The perks of marriage!' quipped Jyotirmayee. Her eyes beamed disgust, as severe as the midday sun. 'Such a shame! What have I got myself into? Is this that same Vijay, that principled, serene man? Oh! What an appalling change! Now I'll have to spend an entire lifetime with him, guilt-stricken like a criminal, shrivelled in a corner of his home. My widowhood was a hundred times, no, a million times preferable. All the sweet fantasies I'd woven have turned bitter. Vijay! Can a leonine soul like him take on the bearings of a sly fox? Over the past month and a half, I've put up with so much, endured such suffering, seeking happiness for this wretched person and myself. I spent eighteen thousand rupees, caused much suffering to Satyanarayan—my manager and my fictional father—and his godlike family too.' So many thoughts and regrets came swarming into her mind.

'How did you get there?' asked Vijay.

'You should ask Virendra,' she replied coldly.

7

Jyotirmayee is now a part of the esteemed Mishra family. Virendra never met Vijay again.

Portrait of a Lady-Love[*]

1

Babu Premkumar was a student of BA at Canning College, Lucknow. He stayed at Mason Hostel. Although the nawabs of Lucknow had long yielded to British rule, Premkumar still sought joy in the breeze that came from Badshah Bagh, the imperial garden. He delighted in the fragrant fairyland of pleasure gardens, spring sunshine, sweet-scented marigold and chirpy bulbuls; in their company, he strolled about peacefully. Possessing a boundless passion for Urdu poetry and deliciously tormented by the pride of a jilted lover, the world he dreamt of thrived a century ago. He had penned a few Urdu couplets, too, which he often recited lounging next to the bathrooms. Whenever a mushaira was organized at his hostel, he made the largest donation; he pored over every page of the magazines, hoping to spot an Urdu poem worthy of his attention. His bond with Hindi,

---

[*] Published as 'Premika Parichay' in *Lili* (1933).

however, went no deeper than a fleeting acquaintance with its alphabet. To him, only those magazines that print Urdu poetry in the Devanagari script were praiseworthy. Meer, Ghalib, Zauq and such: he had committed their poems to his memory, anthology after anthology, hailing Dagh as the doyen among the poets. Residents of the hostel addressed him as Nawab Sahib. Come to think of it, most of the hostellers, barring maybe one or two, were nawabs in their own right. But in the realm of reputation, Premkumar's stature had risen the highest for a reason—in spite of having failed the same class for five years on the trot, his spirit remained undefeated.

Since he hailed from an affluent family, he had come to Lucknow to discover sophistication and urban etiquette, as is the custom these days. It is precisely to further these ends that he spent most of his time around the Chowk—the liveliest market of old Lucknow—which, in turn, is the reason he had cut himself off from textbooks altogether. However, only two signs of the modern times were discernible on his person: the first was his hair, which was fashioned in keeping with the English style of the day; and the second, his boots. Everything else—achkan, pajama, cap, demeanour and the florid Urdu he spoke—bore distinct resemblance to the 'national' dress and the comportment popular with the members of the Hindustani Academy and the Lingua Indica. He often rescued friends lost at the ports of English learning and steered them to the safety of the Eden of the nawabs. Once there, having ensured that the rescued soul is abundantly exposed to the decadent pleasures of the old world, he forced them to admit that other than the chikara—the musical instrument most loved during the days of the nawabs—no instrument ever crafted by human hands can truly blend with the human voice; the chikara comes closest to our natural craving for harmony and culture, he strongly believed. Compared to it, the English clarinet sounds like a braying donkey. Because of these remarkable qualities, Babu Premkumar was a favourite among the students and a subject of ceaseless gossip. Often, quite unprompted, he climbed over the high wall of prohibition—imaginatively, of course, in the tradition of the Chhayavadi poets—and struck wordless conversations with the girls in his class. As expected, the students followed his frolics with unabated interest.

At the hostel, the room adjacent to Premkumar's belonged to Shankar, a Brahmin's son. In spite of the corrupting influence of an English education, he had remained steadfast in defending the customs that have continued unsullied for generations. His father owned a factory that produces soap and tobacco, and had amassed a fortune worth several lakhs of rupees. To ensure his son acquired an English education in addition to his hereditary zeal for protecting Sanatan Dharma, the concerned father packed Shankar off to Lucknow. The noble son had taken after his father— showing high intelligence when it came to defending dharma and observing considerable restraint when it comes to spending money, both in equal measure. He was also skilled at managing his thick plait, which, after a few nifty twists, shapes up as a topknot. He often argued that his style of doing the topknot is, in fact, a technique used to preserve vital electricity in the human body—a method invented by the noble Aryans. Once a classmate of Premkumar, he had now graduated to MA (final)—two years ahead of his hostel mate. For the past three years, Premkumar had been trying hard to civilize Shankar by casting him in his own mould. However, thus far, Shankar had proven to be little more than the blind poet Surdas's black sack: that which admits no light. While Premkumar would gladly take everyone— humans or beasts alike—across the lofty gates of Muslim culture, Shankar displayed comparable gusto in being a sentinel to the narrow lanes of the Aryan civilization, letting none except the Brahmins through.

It is because of these uncongenial traits that Premkumar loved sharing tales of his romances with Shankar; the plan was to soften Shankar till he melted and began to trace the path that Premkumar treaded on. In the time it takes for a season to change, Premkumar scripted at least two or three new love stories. And all this while, he also kept working on Shankar, trying to mellow him with his own version of Raga Malkauns—the celestial melody invented by Saraswati to pacify an inflamed Shiva—and turn him into a lovelorn Baiju Bawara, sounding his cymbals. However, owing to his congenital disposition, Premkumar had started relishing his own descriptions of the beguiling world of lust and longings, much more than Shankar ever did. And why shouldn't he? The sensuous world is, after all, instantly energizing, extremely hypnotizing and, above all, the closest to human nature.

But Shankar lacked the courage to take the road recommended to him; living in constant fear of dharma, he had grown to be a real coward. Whenever Premkumar narrated accounts of the following variety . . .

Today, Miss 'C' asked me out to Sikandar Bagh. What to do? It's rude to turn down someone's heartfelt entreaties; I had to oblige. You know, she completely adores me. As soon as we met, she started saying, 'Tell me, aren't you mine forever?' Such passionate love is not meant to be spurned! Oh, how do I describe what all followed, the things we conversed about! From there, we went straight to the Carlton Hotel, ate and made merry till midnight.

. . . Shankar felt as if he had been pounded—like a mortar under a plummeting pestle— and his desires were aroused wildly. But the lessons his father had taught him, and the fear of losing his caste status, prevented the tempest in his head from raging any more severely. However, by the time he calmed himself down, chanting the Lord's soothing name—'Ram, Ram'—Premkumar attacked his convalescing mind with details of yet another rendezvous.

'Yesterday, I received a letter from Miss Leelavati. None in Lucknow can rival her beauty; I say that with complete conviction. Oh, those mesmerizing eyes! And when she looks at you, she doesn't just see but cuts your heart open. She had asked me to come to Victoria Park, at eight in the night. Look at me; it's nothing but the sheer magic of this fine-looking face. If you desire success in the world, first work on your features. I'll tell you something: with your grim countenance—that expression of misery dancing on your face—even your wife will have no love for you. This face of yours does not merit love. Anyway, back to the story: and then Leelavati and I covered a lot of ground together, if you know what I mean.'

Shankar could feel blood racing through his veins. Over the next five to ten days, he would keep his gaze lowered and his spine erect, and try hard to rein in his throbbing heart. But by the time he sensed any calm, another of Premkumar's stories assailed him. This is how he had spent the last three years in Lucknow.

Of the four types of women mentioned in the scriptures—the best, the middling, the lowly and the pathetic—he had tried his luck with the first three but could never muster enough grit for the ultimate descent. He did make an effort, though, but only once. Meanwhile, Premkumar's ability to describe his lady-loves had sharpened; he had progressed from being subtle to offering full-fledged accounts. Earlier, he would merely try to entice Shankar with the vividness of his descriptions. However, of late, he had also started producing documentary evidence of his exploits.

Shankar had learnt from Premkumar that while talking to women, young or old, one must look directly into their eyes. He had also learnt about the degree of civility desirable in one's tone, the words and the expressions one ought to use, and the manner of their usage too. One day, seizing a moment of solitude, he put these lessons to test on a girl from his own class, only to fail miserably. 'Miss,' he had said. But that simple straightforward address—the word Miss—had enraged the girl into spouting such fire from her eyes that he could never bring himself to look at another 'Miss' for fear of being rusticated from the college.

2

The other day, Premkumar met Shankar excitedly, a letter in his hands. He flung the letter, still enveloped, on to Shankar's bed and said, 'Read what's written here.'

Shankar did his bidding. Written originally in English, the following was its content:

Premkumar, my darling,

For many days now, whenever I am in college, I make sure to steal a glance at your face—at least once. And on the days that I don't, I feel lacerated by the fire of passion that rages inside my heart. But look at you: you are always so cold; never returning my gaze of love, not even mistakenly. It seems God has blessed you with handsome looks just so you can torment me. And here I am, craving something which is not mine to have. Alas! I know you'll laugh at me for saying this, but if, perchance, you don't, I'll thank my stars. Do tell me: Am I entitled to hope that one day you will let me quench the fire that scorches me? You must, dear; I beg you, you must. There is nothing that I ask of you, not a thing in this entire ephemeral world. But I long for that fire—your dazzling face that sets me ablaze. Pray, give it to me, just once, and behold how I surrender my entire being to its leaping flames, turning to ashes right before your eyes. Darling, my hands are beginning

to fail me; I can write no further. Tears stream down
my cheeks. What more can I say? Tomorrow evening,
can you come to Banarasi Bagh—once, just once—and
sate the thirst that ravages my limbs? I'll remain forever
indebted to you, from the depth of my heart. Uff!

The one who could not meet you

Yours,

Shanti

Having read the letter several times over, Shankar
remarked, 'Brother, this reads like the desperate plea of
a pure heart.'

'Doesn't it?' added Premkumar, his head held high.
'I have often advised you that if you can't do much, at least
work a little on your face, make it look like a gentleman's.
But you are one stubborn rustic!'

'I wonder where she came to notice you. You know,
at times, I'm really surprised,' Shankar added, his voice
betraying suspicion.

'What do you mean where? At one of my usual haunts,
I suppose. She must have followed me on the road, got
off her carriage once I stopped and sent the tongawallah
quietly after me, to confirm the address.'

'Really? Is that even possible?'

'You are such a moron. This is Lucknow. Anything is
possible. Besides, when a person truly craves something,
the presiding deity of hearts illuminates the way forward.
However, it's also possible that she used an entirely different
strategy to find out where I lived. You see, she appears to
be a student of a girls' college. And, as you know, I am
extremely popular among the college maidens.'

'But how come all of them end up choosing you at their *swayamvar*?' Shankar demanded to know, visibly exasperated.

'Look this way, here, at my face. They don't choose me, they fall for this handsome face of mine. You won't find features so regal elsewhere, not in all of Lucknow.'

Shankar looked up at Premkumar and broke into a hearty laugh. Premkumar was a Kayasth. The shades of his hair and skin differed only marginally. While the daily use of oil, soap, powder and safety razors cleansed the dirt off his face, it caused his ink-hued skin to glisten even more, like a pair of well-varnished boots. And the thick coating of white powder, which Premkumar spread generously over the shiny black surface, held the beholders captive to its allure.

'Why do you laugh?' inquired Premkumar, peeved.

'Because your argument is so sound that it leaves no space for doubts, not even a teensy bit. You really are firm on meeting her, aren't you?'

'I deem it my duty. The hearts that overflow with love become softer than wax. They can't withstand even the smallest flame. They melt and perish. But how would you know anything about this?'

'You speak the truth. If I were to get such an invitation, first of all, I wouldn't have the courage to accept it. However, even if I somehow nerve myself to do so, only God can predict how the meeting might end. I doubt if Goddess Saraswati would let my feelings rise to my lips.'

At this, Premkumar guffawed and invoked a maxim in English: 'The face is the index of the mind. Besides, I am sure you'll never be asked out. However, if you shun your

Brahmanical orthodoxy, I may, in good time, manage to groom you into a sociable creature.'

3

By early evening, Premkumar was at Banarasi Bagh, his carriage parked by the road. Deer, rhino, cheetah, lion, birds, ostriches, kangaroo, tiger, bear, wolf, zebra and donkey—he saw all the animals, hopping from cage to cage, fence to fence, desperate to discover the one he had come to meet. But he couldn't have discovered the beloved himself. How could he? Rather, he was meant to be 'found' by her. Yet, whenever a sari-clad beauty came into sight—her supple body swaying like a flame—and appeared to walk towards him, he, too, took a step or two in her direction, his stride exuding confidence. But on each occasion, much before he could come anywhere near the lady, he was greeted with words of reproach hurled at him by her friends or, on a few occasions, by the lady's male companion. 'What an imbecile! Does he not have eyes?' And every time, his advancing feet would freeze midway.

It felt as if hope had turned its back on him. For four hours, he kept loitering about the park. On one or two occasions, even the tongawallahs came up to him, suspecting a potential passenger, but went back disappointed. Whenever he stumbled upon a group of young women, sitting and absorbed in chatting, he started hovering around them, hoping to get recognized. Gradually, the place got deserted, but Premkumar refused to give up; he kept circling the park, walking along its boundary wall. Yet he could not find his Shanti. Having lost his other *shanti*, i.e., his peace of mind, he dragged his listless frame to the waiting carriage, reached his hostel and stretched himself quietly in the bed.

The following day, when Shankar came over to Premkumar's room to check on him, he witnessed a shrivelled face. This has to be the hangover of *prem*, or love, manifesting itself so morosely on Premkumar's countenance, thought Shankar. He beheld his friend with adoring eyes and asked, 'Brother, how did the first encounter with your lady-love go?' Having demanded the details, Shankar sat next to Premkumar, eager and animated.

'Of the many reasons why India has fallen into disrepute, this one stands out: we make a thousand promises, but fail to honour even a few. This is why the leash of slavery refuses to fall from our necks. If a society burdened with these many awful habits hopes for social and political reformation, would that ever happen?' observed Premkumar, his annoyance vividly evident.

'Oh, so it turned out to be a day of broken promise. Hadn't I warned you that someone might be pranking you? But for you all and sundry are Yudhisthira incarnate—truth personified.'

'Well, such is my trusting nature: I take others to be as cultured and noble-hearted as myself. I could never imagine that such an uncivilized girl may come to exist in Lucknow, that too amid the dignified tribe of educated city women.'

'Oh, it's a heart-breaking betrayal; left my mood completely soured,' grumbled Shankar, casting a look of insolence at his friend.

Just then, a mailman came into sight. Premkumar followed his movements closely. Indeed, the mailman was headed towards him. He walked up to them and delivered an envelope. As Premkumar opened the letter and read it, an instant bout of happiness washed over him. 'See, we were so wrong about her. Look at this: it is the portrait of an untainted heart,' said Premkumar, pointing at the letter, his face flushed with pride.

Shankar took it and started reading. It said:

Prem, the Lord of my being,

Such troubles you had to endure yesterday, all because of me! While you were scampering across the compounds in the zoo, getting impatient for your Shanti, I was at the open ground across from the bus stand, escorted by my mother and laughing at your misery, whenever you flashed past us. How I wished I could run to you, tell you about your Shanti, insist on a reward for the priceless information and force you to agree to my demand. But I couldn't; my mother was with me all this while. She was the reason we couldn't get together. But do you have any inkling of those countless occasions when I have been with you? So many times, in so many ways, with my eyes, with my heart, with my words and with my boundless love. I am the same person who had once mesmerized you, whose silent entreaties had moved your soul, whose sight had forced you to stop, transfixed, whose absence had left you bereft. I want you to feel the intense heat of the fire that you have lit in your beloved's heart. And realize the depths of her desperation, for even though she had put the strength of your love to the toot, she couldn't come to you herself. Alas! All the pain you had to quietly bear for me! Trust me, you'll get your Shanti. Please be kind and come to the Elphinstone cinema tomorrow. You must, I beseech you. You must!

Hewitt Road, Lucknow
4-4-32

Yours,
Shanti

'Yaar, her letter is pure poetry,' Shankar observed, smiling.

'Indeed, she seems like a well-educated girl. And she writes such sophisticated English too,' said Premkumar, struggling to conceal his pride. 'But if one's mother is around, could one lay bare one's heart and speak freely?'

'The lady belongs to an illustrious family, I reckon,' Shankar added, heaping exaggerated praise on her.

'Indeed. These aren't the manners of a girl from a house of ragamuffins. You see, maidens from distinguished families are often compared to grass: their heart, like the stem of a grass leaf, remains moist and tender, even when they wilt under the blazing sun for twelve long years. That's how they manage to stay alive. And when a kind soul pours a little water on them, or when the sky drizzles a bit, they bloom back to life, four times as lush and gushing over the one who has brought water. And what's more, they instantly repay their debt of gratitude, soothing the eyes of the benefactor with their verdant beauty.'

'You speak so truthfully. Are you planning to go to the movie theatre?' Shankar asked, his tone betraying a hint of insistence.

'Did you hear me say "I won't"? If a man gets an invite, that too from such an exalted family, and he turns it down, it is, to my mind, the gravest insolence imaginable in the world,' said Premkumar, putting a new safety-blade in his razor and taking a position in front of the mirror placed on the table.

'One must go, unfailingly. To tell you the truth, I, too, desire her darshan, but only after you have met her. She must be good at writing poems in English.'

'Yes, she has the soul of a true poet. Each line of her verse tugs at one's heartstrings. Doesn't it?'

'Tug hard. My friend, truth be told, her poems inflict wounds on your body, but it is I who wriggle in pain.'

'They are so perfectly crafted that if you erase so much as one word, the whole poem begins to limp,' said Premkumar, lathering his beard, lost in the beauty of the beloved's poetry.

'Let me meet her first. I'll introduce you to her after that, I promise. This is how you will gradually evolve into a civilized man. The world today has marched far ahead of your Brahminical ideas. Besides, you are an educated man, you ought to reason yourself. And as far as I am concerned, I firmly believe in the absolute freedom to socialize with the members of the opposite sex, and maybe do much more, afterwards.'

4

It was six in the morning. There was a small crowd outside Elphinstone Picture Palace. The film *Shailbala*, being screened at the theatre, was reportedly a hit. The paanwallahs, roguish young men from both Hindu and Muslim families, and the poor of the city—all crammed chock-a-block in narrow queues—were advancing slowly towards the ticket windows, buying tickets worth four and eight annas. Several cars were parked nearby. For quite a while, Premkumar milled about the place. He looked admiringly at the film posters—the one currently showing and the one upcoming, both. He then turned to the images of Sulochana, Zubeida, Madhuri, Kajjan, Mushtari, Sheela, Kapoor and Mukhtar Begum, even though their photos were already in his room, treasured with care. In fact, he had got Zubeida's portrait done with an expensive golden-bordered frame—fitted with a reclining stand of the kind that supports mirrors—and had displayed it proudly on his table. But today, he hung around those familiar faces and posters for a special reason: if Shanti came, he would get to meet her before the show begins and also find out about the class to which she had bought her ticket. It would be reckless to buy the ticket without that key information; this, he understood well. What if Shanti got into a different class and the chance to meet her slipped by?

Meanwhile, whenever a man walked past him, holding hands with his young wife, a ticklish sensation coursed through his body, for he mistook the couple to be Shanti and her father. And then the young woman would cast a withering glance at him, laced with unspoken disgust and reproach. But unscathed by the bitter experience, Premkumar got ready for his next ambush.

With only two minutes left for the show to begin, panic set in. He concluded that Shanti had already entered the hall by the time he had reached the venue, and now her famished eyes must be seeking him out in the crowd. The thought made him restless; he could not decide where or to which class he should go to. She must be seated somewhere inside, saying his name on beads. But how was he supposed to locate her? Finally, a decision was made: it was preferable to step inside rather than wait outside. He produced his college library card at the ticket counter and bought a balcony ticket at a discounted rate. When he stepped in, the lights were out and the show had started. He had hoped to scan through the theatre— all around, as far as his eyes could see—but the darkness broke his heart.

As the film progressed, his anxiety deepened. While others concentrated on the story unfolding on the screen, he could only think of Shanti, picturing her in his mind's eye. Trapped alone in the mist of that nothingness, he tried to recall her words. 'Her letter said that she has seen me and that I have seen her too. Let me think: which of the girls was I most attracted to? Could she be that one—that fair lady? No, it can't be her. When I had looked at her, I could hear someone abuse me. Or maybe those words weren't meant for me. She was taking some eve-teaser to task.'

It was already an hour into the show, but Premkumar had no inkling of the images flashing across the screen; he was single-mindedly thinking about Shanti.

A bell rang announcing the interval, and the lights came on. Premkumar inspected the entire theatre thoroughly—from the topmost row to the one at the bottom—and saw many girls seated all around him, each more beautiful than the other. The whole setting was so baffling that he couldn't figure whom to approach. There was no way to ascertain which of them was Shanti. Could she be the prettiest one? He started examining each one of them closely. And every time his roving eyes stopped at a beauty—her eyes, clothes, shape, chin and face, every feature awash in the bright light—he was convinced that her loveliness had no parallel. Whoever he took a fancy to, he thought of as Shanti. Oh, what a terrible crisis! Which of them is the prettiest? His mind refused to brood over such an unfair question. There were as many types of visage as there were women—round, oblong, square, even—each a beauty in her own right, each radiating sweet innocence.

He felt thoroughly exhausted after all the stressful work. Although he could gladly go on admiring the beauties, his mind felt too tired to focus on the crucial question of Shanti's identity. Nevertheless, he thought of a strategy. 'Shanti has to be among them. It is in the nature of every woman to consider herself the most alluring of all beauties, and Shanti cannot be an exception to this universal rule. Assuming she is right about herself, at the end of the show, simply stand by the road and look at each of the pretty ones passing by. You must have seen her, without fail,' he told himself.

At long last, the show came to an end. Premkumar emerged from the theatre and started sauntering about the road, masculine pride playing on his face. But Shanti was nowhere to be found. The many giggling Shantis who walked down the road—holding their husbands' hands and quite outspoken in their criticism of *Shailbala*—scorched him with envy. Dejected but still trying to warm his heart with a flickering sense of hope, he mounted a tonga and asked the driver to take him to Badshah Bagh.

On reaching Badshah Bagh, he took to dismantling the idol of his beloved—once treasured more than his own life—with the ferocious strength of a giant. But the broken pieces came together, as if forming atomic bonds and drawing energy from his very soul. They coalesced into many striking forms: these were the shapes of the sweet faces that he had studied carefully a short while ago and that had berated him with their fiery eyes. But gradually, his vision got blurred, as if held hostage by the sorcery of the demoness Marichika, and he started imagining Shanti's face in each of those seductive visages. But that was all he could do; hopeless and clueless, he boarded the tonga, got down at the hostel, paid the fare and quietly slunk into his room.

5

Next morning, Shankar decided against meeting Premkumar; he did not wish to waste his valuable time so early in the day. Premkumar himself was too perplexed to walk over to Shankar's room. However, once back from the college, Shankar tried to gauge the situation, albeit without stepping into his friend's room. Premkumar seemed happy; he was humming a popular ghazal, which the students of Canning College had jestingly labelled as the national song of Lucknow. It went:

If fate had decreed that I be a necklace, around the beloved's neck hung,

The envious world would have called me an eyesore, a source of irritation.

Shankar realized that either Premkumar's luck had finally smiled on him or he had received a new letter, with instructions for yet another meeting the following day. Finally, he walked into his room, a mischievous smile playing on his face, and asked excitedly, 'Well, brother, at last you did meet your lady-love, didn't you?'

'A wise man has rightly said: the ecstasy that I felt in separation was lost somewhat in union,' philosophized Premkumar.

'Ah, so your days of waiting aren't over yet?' asked Shankar, a little surprised.

'The thing is: yesterday, I went for the first show, while she came for the second. So we couldn't meet. And now she sends this letter, hurling taunts at me. Take this.'

Shankar took the letter held out to him and started going through it:

Dearest Prem,

Yesterday, I went for the second show, but you were nowhere to be found. What is this funny business? Are you upset with me? Please do forgive me, if you are indeed angry with me. But think about this: How was I at fault? You came for the first show, you got it wrong. Tell me something: Is it at all possible for

lovelorn hearts to unite during the day's first show?
Had you come for the second, we would have stayed
out for the entire length of the film, strolled along the
Gomati, gossiping all the while, and once the show was
over, I would have returned home. During the morning
show, the town is so full of bustle; lovers like us can
hardly steal a private movement. And since you did go
to the first show after all, I am assuming you would
have ogled at those demonic witches at the theatre and
thought I was one of them. Oh! How badly you have
insulted me! But a promise is a promise; it's time we
honoured our pact. Tomorrow, you must wait for me
by the bank of the Gomati, under the Chotelal Bridge,
an open umbrella in hand. I'll come for a bath. You will
have a clear sight of me; that way, I'll be etched in your
mind, and you won't get to forget me ever. And then
someday, somewhere, we'll be together. Tomorrow,
you'll certainly meet your Shanti; have no doubt. I'll be
at the women's ghat, sharp at eight.

Your long-lost Shanti

Reading the letter, Shankar felt his spirits lift. 'I must say,
lady luck is sure to smile on you now.'

'Hope there are no more unexpected hiccups to upset
my plan. They ruin even clinched deals,' said Premkumar,
his voice filled with serene happiness.

'These early troubles should be welcomed—they make
the final success feel grander, taste sweeter, particularly
when the matter concerns love. I can already feel some

of that joy, quite palpably so,' said Shankar, looking contentedly at the letter.

'It is said that a musk melon puts on the colour of the nearest melon on the farm. You, my friend, are the same as a musk melon. Now tell me, whose august company do you keep, day in, day out? Fortunately, at long last, you have managed to put on the shades of your illustrious companion. That's why your idea of love has become so vivid,' said Premkumar, exuding supreme self-contentment.

6

Next day, Premkumar was up and about by five in the morning. At six he headed out towards the Chotelal Bridge, bathed and fashionably dressed, twirling an umbrella. For the next two hours, till eight, he simply bided his time: standing idly, squatting without need and loitering aimlessly along the bank of the Gomati. Time flew by— eight made way for nine, and nine marched into ten—but no one walked up to him to say, 'Dear, you've fretted a great deal for my sake. Meet me: I am your Shanti.' Only a sharp-tongued stranger approached him and spoke discourteously, 'I've been noticing you loitering about this place for much too long now, and how you ogle at every woman that comes your way. I was wondering when you stare like that, so shamelessly, aren't you ever reminded of your own mother or sister at home?'

Sin induces cowardice. Premkumar couldn't find the courage to respond. His face fell. Quietly, he limped up the steps leading out of the ghat, took the road to Badshah

Bagh, reached his hostel and crashed on his bed. That day, he skipped all his meals. In his heart of hearts, Premkumar was strengthening his resolve to penalize Shanti. But just then, the mailman arrived, right at his designate time, and gave him a note. It read:

O Lord of the fools,

Didn't you find water enough in the Gomati to drown yourself?

Yours,
Shanti

5 Hewitt Road,
Lucknow

It shook him up badly. A little later, Shankar came over too. The letter was still on the table, open and abandoned. Shankar read it too. 'Yaar, this is such a vulgar prank. You must go to 5 Hewitt Road and find out who lives there,' said Shankar, struggling to repress his laughter.

Premkumar had a newly married sister-in-law who lived near Hewitt Road with her husband. She was a student in Premkumar's own college—previously his batch mate, but now a senior research scholar. When Kshama saw him at her doorstep, she burst into laughter. 'You are such an idiot. Shanti is Didi's name, according to her horoscope.'

What I Saw[*]

1

There is a police station next to the press, where the brokers of peace live and thrive. If you ever wish to marvel at the sight of Hindu–Muslim camaraderie, with your eyes wide open, just look out of the window to the western wall of our building. As for us, we behold this spectacle of matchless love day and night. What's all the more praiseworthy is the fact that this love is not restricted to humans; it's easily discernible among the animals and birds of the locality, too. The pet dogs of the Hindus and the chickens of the Muslims also love each other.

Right there, on the platform around the peepal tree, an abode of Lord Bhootnath has been set up. While the average devotees of Lord Shiva—hoping to fulfil

---

[*] Originally published as 'Kya Dekha'. This was Nirala's first story, serialized in 1922 in the monthly *Matwala*.

their ambition of world conquest—try to propitiate the Lord with a modest offering of only four grains of rice, the generous Hindus of the locality are known to offer forty-four grains. But the bold chickens peck away all the offerings, clutching Shivji with their claws, as goons clutch those whom they exact protection money from. Pleased with the feed, the chickens then look skywards and let out a joyous crow—*kukdookoo*—beseeching Allah to make the Hindus conquerors of the world.

* * *

That night, I didn't get any sleep. When dawn broke, I quickly got up, sat leaning against a table beside the bed and began reflecting hard on the things that had recently befallen me. It's an incident of epic proportions, encompassing all the known rasas—from the erotic to the odious. Just then, a thought occurred to me:

'Is her love true, or is it a lie? What if it's just playacting? If it were so, why did she turn down the millionaires prepared to not just sweat but also bleed for her sake? The poor folks went back dejected, their faces fallen. If she's indeed a prostitute, why didn't she favour a patron with deep pockets? Come to think of it, this could also be the handiwork of an enemy who had hatched an ingenious plot to trap me. But her voice, dripping with sadness, did not betray any deception; it didn't ring of feminine deceitfulness. Regardless, I will stick to my refusal to meet her, right till the very end. Aesthetics be damned! The pursuit of beauty took me to a brothel in the company of poet Sundarlal and made me learn its first principles at the feet of a prostitute.'

As I was grappling with these thoughts, a cock almost shattered my ears with its cacophonous crow. Rudely startled, I lost my chain of thoughts.

2

It was about ten in the morning when a letter arrived. It was meant for Sundarlalji. A servant had left it on the table. Even though the letter was addressed to him, not me, it had been sent to me for a reason. It read as follows:

13, New Street, Calcutta 3-9-23

Dearest Sundarji,

Do come over this evening and bring along that friend of yours—the one who'd accompanied you last Wednesday. This is my fervent plea. What more can I say?

Yours truly,
Hira

From the little that was written in the letter, one could readily gather the surface meaning. But it wasn't enough to grasp the lurking subtext. My poor brain, already possessed by suspicion, started loafing down the twisted alleys of my warped imagination. Much as I tried, I could not put a leash on my mutinous mind. Tell me, what else could I have done? Back then, I felt no more in control of my life than a hired mule—my mind, mounted on the beast of burden, took it wherever it wanted. If only I had submitted unquestioningly to the pursuit of beauty and agreed to sit through a few minutes of mujra, as the goddess of beauty had demanded, I would've been spared those hours of indecision; I would've been at peace. But my own anxiety about societal approbation stood blocking my path, like the feet of the monkey–prince Angad, planted immovably in Ravan's durbar. Yet, my stubborn heart kept hurling provocative questions at me. Why is it impossible? Why can't the two pursuits—of beauty and brahmcharya—go together? But my contradictory self mocked me with sarcasm: Well, go ahead, enjoy the mujra. What's there to fear? As the poets suggest, 'Swim irresolutely and sink, swim heartily and sail.' If you can't commit fully to an idea, you had better stay away from it.

The thoughts of rumour-mongering enemies and my deep veneration for the fairer sex dissuaded me from accepting the invitation. At the same time, my love of poetry, music, the arts, sublime skills, feminine grace— the whole gamut of allurements that the world of beauty conjured up—slackened the leash of self-restraint, emboldening me to make my move. To lead my mind away from the temptation, I recited quatrains from the Ramayana, the ones that I could recall. But alas, they too failed to sober me up. The God of etiquette, absorbedly weaving a colourful yarn on my mind's spinning wheel, paid no attention to the pious tunes. Desperate, I thought of reaching out to Sundarlalji. Perhaps his intervention could salvage the situation. Otherwise, my dinghy was sure to capsize in those troubled waters.

Braving the blistering summer sun on my naked head, I somehow scurried through the mile-long road. Sundarlal was busy writing, sitting quietly in the library. The moment he saw me, he put aside his pen and teased me smilingly, 'Ah, such impatience! We have a full six hours to while away.'

'What's the matter, Sundarlalji? I don't get it at all. I barely know her, and yet she's after my life. Please save me,' I blurted it all out in a single breath.

'Dear Sir, is she a tigress threatening to devour you alive? If she so insists, there's no harm in coming along. It won't sully your fine reputation. Attending mujra is a common practice in this city and, in my opinion, useful for literary pursuits too.'

'No, please rescue me from her claws.'

'Off with your hypocrisy! Just don't go. However, it is said that all our mighty poets—from Kalidasa till today—when afflicted with writer's block, found the company of women somewhat healing. You're but a young novice. This wisdom will come to you much later.'

To retort was to deepen my own wound. Hence I decided to return to my place.

3

Sundarlal reached Hira's house right on time. There were quite a few chairs laid out in the lounge area. He wasted no time lowering himself into one of those. Upon noticing Sundarlal, Hira's *bandi*, the maid-in-waiting, swayed to the adjacent room to inform her mistress of the guest's arrival. The walls of the lounge were decked with several portraits, mostly of Hira in action—singing, dancing and such. In one of the frames she was dressed as a man. One could easily tell that Sundarlal was captivated by that striking image. He ogled at it with piercing eyes and kept scribbling something in his notebook, as if collecting material for a poem.

Having gathered the necessary information from the *bandi*, Hira finally appeared in the lounge. The rays of blatant importunity that Sundarlal's eyes beamed out fell all over her graceful visage. However, upon being intercepted by the shield of annoyance she had come armed with, those rays got scattered away. The amorous dreams forged in Sundarlal's lovesick heart took turns to greet Hira. But meeting her stubborn indifference, each recoiled in shame, as a bashful young bride recoils at the sight of her husband's elder brother, her shy face enveloped in a ghoonghat. Like a fly crazed by a flame, Sundarlal wanted to lose himself in Hira's fiery beauty. But it seemed shielded by a glass wall of restraint; much as he tried, he could not reach for it.

For nearly three minutes, Hira stood still, as if she had braced herself for the onslaught. Finding the sea so menacingly calm, a fisherman can sense an impending storm. The thundering had stopped, the wind had slowed down, and the clouds were packed tightly, with no gap left to gaze at the blue sky that lay beyond. The signs were clear—it was going to pour down in torrents.

'Sundarlalji,' uttered Hira peevishly, but then restrained herself in no time. Her feelings were eager to burst forth through her words. But she had mastered the art of reining in her emotions and putting on a disguise. To many an irritating fool, she had sung Sohni or the peasants' songs of weeding, instead of Sahaana, the wedding songs celebrating love, and earned rewards too.

'I see your friend hasn't come,' she said calmly. Her tone was neither too desperate nor too indifferent. And what is more, she didn't even allow Sundarlal time enough to examine its import. She hurriedly presented him with a betel box, her manners painted as earlier. Puffed by his sense of superiority, Sundarlal accepted the offering gleefully and explained, 'He said he was scared of slander. As for me, I don't consider him much of a human being. He is but a semi-literate moron.'

Hira's probing eyes were fixed intently on Sundarlal, as if trying to skim out the truth from a pool of lies. The word 'slander' echoed in her heart. For a short while, she appeared unconcerned.

'When will your singing start? The musicians are still missing.' Sundarlal sounded curious.

'Perhaps there may not be any singing today. The accompanists are at Pukhraj's place. Besides, I don't feel so well either. If I knew your friend is so shallow, I would've never invited him. It seems he had mistakenly wandered into my home the other day. By the way, where does he live?'

'Here, in Calcutta,' answered Sundarlal.

'Ah, must be near the garbage dumping ground,' added Hira with a roguish smile.

'No, no, he lives in quite a respectable locality—3 Grey Street. He is a man of good taste.'

'I don't think I can sing today. I am a bit unwell. When I learnt of your arrival, I somehow pulled myself out of bed just to welcome you. I had been resting until then.'

'Not a problem, not a problem! Please rest well,' purred Sundarlal.

Hira wasn't remiss in her courtesies while seeing him off; she stood smiling by the window for as long as Sundarlal was in sight. Once he was gone, she was swift to note down the address: 3 Grey Street.

4

Several weeks had passed since the incident. Meanwhile, Sundarlal's friend had taken ill. But for the past two days he had been on the mend. Sitting in his bed he was wrestling with his thoughts.

'Even though I sent for him, not once did Sundarlal bother to visit me while I was sick. Whenever my servant went to fetch him, he would be ready with an excuse. If he's angry, I can't seem to fathom why. Let me first get well, then I'll find out why he's so cross with me. A bosom friend turning a blind eye during days of crisis is a cause for concern. But that young Sikh fellow, Amar Singh, who visited me all through my sickness, seems like a good friend. And a man of firm resolve too. Each evening, he summoned the doctor unfailingly, carried my prescription to the market, brought me medicines and, before leaving, thoroughly instructed my servant to be on time with the doses. How he amuses with his conversations, how full of news and gossip he always is. It seems he reads a lot of newspapers. It's evening again. He'll be here any moment now.'

Bhajna was worried by that somber look he noticed on his employer's face; he could not muster up the courage to break the news. More than once, he steeled his nerves and braved forward, but each time grew nervous and stopped. Outside the house, Amar Singh's patience caved in.

'What is it, Bhajna? Is Babuji asleep? If so, pull aside his blanket and wake him up. Today he's been served his first proper meal since he took ill. But instead of sitting upright for a while to help his digestion, he decides to lie down,' complained Amar Singh. Even though his voice was thin, his bearing was all masculine bluster.

Amar Singh's voice was like a knock at the door of distress—so loud a knock that the presiding deity of anguished brains was compelled to take heed of it and worm out of an earhole for an audience. When the thus-alerted master cast his gaze at his help's elephantine gait, he could not help asking a few stern questions. 'What's the matter with you? Is this how you walk? Or are you trying to measure the floor with your steps? Since when did you acquire this ceremonial stride?'

'Since the day you took to building castles in the air,' Bhajna wanted to snipe at his employer. But sadly, by now he had inculcated the courtesies observed in polite circles. And so he gulped down his wild, freedom-bred words, as one swallows one's saliva, and produced a lame, prosaic reply, 'Amar Singhji has been waiting for long.'

'For long? Don't you dare stop him any longer.'

5

Even though Amar Singh was a Sikh, he wasn't all that tall. Perhaps other Indians may not find his height out of character, but the Sikhs shall surely consider him a dwarf. However, what he lacked in height he made up for with his extraordinarily long hair. An average Sikh may have had an arm's length of height advantage over him, but when it came to the strands on his head, he remained unmatched in his entire community, with a minimum lead of two arms' length. Even though I never bothered asking whether the brave young man felt burdened by his thick, lustrous hair, I could not help noticing how his fair-complexioned face— beautiful as the moon—appeared sunk under his silken turban. It was so bulbous it seemed as if an entire length of cloth was draped around his head.

As soon as Amar Singh walked in, he inquired after me. 'So, sahab, how do you feel today?'

'Better. How do I express my gratitude to you? I can't seem to find the right words. I'm forever indebted to you,' replied Pyarelal.

'For now, keep your gratitude nicely treasured. But in the space of a few days, you'll surely forget all about it. And then, you'll be content to look the other way when you see me, as if you've never known me. I tell the truth. In my life, however short it's been, I've seen many shades of the world. Please be grateful to none but God, whose grace has healed you,' he declaimed.

'We all are always grateful to Him—whether times are kind or harsh. Truth be told, invoking His mercy has become more of a fad. Much like a convenient catchphrase. But no one has seen God. We've only heard of him. Yet, by and by, we find ourselves tied down by the sturdy ropes of religion. I call it a vice. If God is guileless, why would he solicit your gratitude? Or be flustered by your oversights? It is unfair to drag Him in each little discussion on good and evil. If there is a force responsible for vices and virtues of the world, it is man himself. Therefore, man alone should be the subject of both condemnation and praise.'

'You speak like a great scholar. To debate God with you is to lay bare my own idiocy. Yet, it is beyond doubt that man is a turncoat. Haven't your philosophers fussed enough over the subject? But let it be. If you start philosophizing, there's no stopping you for hours. At the moment, your body is frail. It might cause your head to heat up. By the way, what name did you mention the other day? I can't seem to recall it.'

'It's a pity that you keep forgetting one simple name,' Pyarelal protested in good humour.

'It is like a *panchladi*—a five-stringed necklace—of Sanskrit words. That's why I prefer to address you by the name I gave you,' Amar Singh reasoned.

'Panchladi. What an interesting word! It brings a feminine touch to our conversation.'

'Oh, so you possess masculinity too? Your face seems to testify to your femininity alone. If your majestic name adds a dash of masculinity to your person, people find your face that much feminine.'

'It's called *lavanya*—unbounded charm. You won't get it,' Pyarelal quipped.

'But only women have use for it. Men seek virile manliness,' Amar Singh countered.

'Perhaps you mistake manliness for a butcher's cruel appearance. If such is the case, then its meaning is lost upon you. A man's face mirrors his innermost feelings. If signs of sternness are absent from my face, it should be assumed that thoughts inimical to humanity never cross my mind. My feelings are noble, and they shine bright on my face.'

'All right. But please be so kind as to tell me your name. And along with it, those beautiful imaginings, too, whose perplexing pursuit has turned your face feminine,' Amar Singh urged.

'My father was a great Sanskrit scholar. He named me Janaki Ballabh Sharan Bihari. But people call me Bihari.'

'But you are a Bihari.'

'Correct. And I am proud of being a Bihari. Just as Bengalis are proud of their Bengali heritage and Madrasis are . . .'

'In other words, there is nothing excitingly new about it. It's just a matter of identity,' Amar Singh teased on.

'However it may be! But I see that the sensation of love flows through every man. In fact, through every living being.'

'That it does. But tell me: Do you see it because it's in abundance, or because as a Bihari you have a special way of looking at things?'

'Serious matters mustn't be belittled through trivial jokes. I can feel that sensation because I indulge in it all the time,' Pyarelal asserted firmly.

'I don't believe you. I think you are lying. You speak of an ideal whose existence you can't credibly establish.'

'Why not? Haven't we been debating its existence all along? The proof lies in the face.'

Amar Singh smiled and turned his face away. 'One's own face can't be its proof. It may be found in another's.' For a moment, their smiling eyes met.

'I'll call you Pyarelal. If I call you Bihari, people might jeer at you,' observed Amar Singh. At that precise moment, his eyes were drawn to the table. A new magazine lay on it. It was *Madhuri*. Amar Singh picked it up and began leafing through it.

'Haven't you subscribed to *Madhuri*?' Pyarelal wanted to know.

'I have,' pat came the reply.

'Then why are you flipping through it?'

'There's a poem I wanted to show you.'

'Which one?'

'This one—the only poem in the current issue.'

'Ah, yes. It's really good. I've read it already,' answered Pyarelal, his eyes glued to the poem in print.

'It's about *viyog shringaar*, love in separation,' Amar Singh boldly summed it up.

'No, I believe these lines express sentiments deeply personal to the poetess. That is why they tug hard at our heartstrings.'

'I can't bring myself to empathize with such crybabies.'

'But it has turned out to be quite an excellent work of art. The sentiments have been forcefully expressed. There are no knotty words that befuddle the meaning. I speak here as a literary critic,' argued Pyarelal.

'I don't think you quite understand the critic in me.'

'Are you fond of satire?'

'To tell you the truth, I like everything, yet nothing. Besides, whoever has understood satire? It's so slippery.'

'Why so?'

'I speak from experience.'

'Are you trying to suggest that satire is beyond me too? Are you trying to suggest I should have proclaimed you omniscient, in words plain and simple?'

'No, it's not a question of omniscience. But one can always distinguish good from bad. This here is a creation of the highest merit.'

'Well, let me have a look at it. Give it to me. I will consult a professor on the subject.'

'Didn't you say you were a subscriber?' Pyarelal asked, sounding suspicious.

'But I'm not carrying this issue with me. On the way back, I'll drop by at my professor's place and take up the matter with him.'

'So you don't trust my judgment? Please tell me, what do you wish to take an expert opinion on? Versification, rasa, metaphors, metre?'

'It appears you would rather take the trouble of explaining everything yourself than part with the magazine.'

'I haven't finished reading it yet.'

'Okay, then tell me: Who is this Hira, the poetess?'

The question made Pyarelal blush. The probing eyes of Amar Singh, waiting keenly for an answer, were fixed on him. 'Never mind. You finish reading it first. I'll pick it up later,' Amar Singh spoke reassuringly.

Pyarelal was left distraught. Amar Singh bade him goodbye.

6

Pyarelal had been in good health for a few days now. Every evening, Amar Singh visited him and the two gossiped leisurely for a while. Of late, Pyarelal was fixated on Amar Singh's face, as much as he was charmed by his selfless solicitude; that visage resembled the image of beauty treasured in Pyarelal's heart. He now associated the same piety with Amar Singh's face that he had previously associated with his kindness. For Pyarelal, the force of these thoughts was both gratifying and elevating. However, little did he realize that his itch to devour piety with naked eyes was gradually unmasking him.

Even though the desire wasn't exactly egregious, it was almost that. It could spell trouble for him; it was like dancing with the devil. It also hacked at the root of his celibacy vow. But Pyarelal remained oblivious to all this. He kept mistaking this lust for beauty for a literary pursuit. His besotted heart snaked out through his eyes and, in its unfulfilled hunger, devoured an external object. When the heart is coiled around something beautiful, it is provoked into rebelling against all things abhorrent. Pyarelal failed to grasp this fact.

For as long as he had Amar Singh's company, he kept staring at his face with rapt fascination. He began secretly admiring him—sometimes his eyes, sometimes his lips, sometimes the sweet things he said that filled his heart with ambrosia, and sometimes the bounteous grace that oozed out of every part of him, adorned lovingly by nature's gentle hands.

One evening, Amar Singh did not show up. Nothing explained his absence. Since Pyarelal had formed a deep bond of friendship with Amar Sing, he waited restlessly. 'He must've been stuck somewhere, but now he's surely on his way,' he consoled himself. However, there was no sign of Amar Singh till ten in the evening. Disappointed, he ate his dinner and went to bed, but didn't get any sleep till late into the night.

Next morning, the newspaper hawker delivered the *Dainik Swatantra*. Its cover page proclaimed, in big bold letters: 'Murder in Eden Garden'.

'A case of double murder.'

'Mr Hague was stabbed in the heart, and Hira was shot in the head.'

Pyarelal was surprised at finding Hira's name in the report. He started reading it with great excitement. It was a brief report that read as follows:

> Mr Hague was the manager of Born and Co., while Hira was a famous courtesan from 13 New Street, Calcutta. The police are investigating the motive behind the murders. When a couple is murdered, people tend to gossip about their characters. It appears to be a case of rape, as Hira was wielding a knife. It seems she had used it at a moment of distress. Before dying, the injured sahib must have shot Hira fatally. His was a seven-bullet revolver, from which one bullet was fired and six were still loaded.

The report rattled Pyarelal; a sensation of shock coursed through his veins, from head to toe. He tried hard to compose himself, but to no avail; his restless mind kept weaving and unravelling imaginary tales around that newspaper report. Emotions of all hues appeared on his face, but he couldn't decide exactly what to feel about the incident. His mind was restless, like a playful little child. Every instinct of his—articulate and latent, subconscious and conscious—rejected the news of Hira's death. His agitated mind rummaged around hopelessly for an answer. Finally, he settled for the theory that it was the sahib's atrocity that had caused the fallout. He also convinced himself of Hira's innocence, picturing intermittently her brave and immaculate conduct in the sad episode. The thought made his heart swell with pride.

Just then, the servant brought a letter. Pyarelal promptly opened it. It read:

Meet me as soon as you find the letter. Howsoever pressing your engagements might be, set them aside and come along with the courier. What more can I say?

Yours,
Amar Singh

The letter was like the flash of lightning one needs to find one's way around in a dark, overcast night. But once the dazzle died out, the surrounding darkness became four times as dense.

Pyarelal set off instantly, not even bothering to change the ordinary daywear he was attired in. The courier led the way, Pyarelal followed. Soon, they found themselves at New Street, having made their way hurriedly through many lanes and roads. There was a signboard near the turn that said 'New Street'. Pyarelal read the words and froze momentarily in fear. But then he composed himself and moved forward. When he found the mailman stepping into Hira's house, he felt taken aback; the sight made no sense to him. But he kept walking mechanically. Just then, a maid came down the stairs and escorted Pyarelal away.

7

There was dead silence all around. A pall of gloom hung heavy over the room. The windows were shut, and everything seemed cloaked under a dark blanket. A young man was sitting on a couch, seemingly absorbed in some thoughts.

As Pyarelal entered the room, his legs began to tremble; he was unnerved by the eerie silence. His body froze in nervousness, his face fell. The young man got up, guided Pyarelal to another couch in the room and then returned to his seat.

Pyarelal: 'Amar Singh?'

Amar Singh: 'Yes.'

Incessant weeping had made Amar Singh's throat sore and his voice hoarse. This alone revealed how deep his sorrow was. But his mourning did not stir any sympathy in Pyarelal's heart; instead, it aroused dark suspicion. He thought of Hira and, for a while, sat brooding. As to what was playing on his mind when he returned to his senses— whether he had thought it through or if his musings were interrupted—I can't say for sure.

'So, Amar Singh, how was Hira murdered? I read about it in today's newspaper. And what brings you here? Did you know Hira?'

The questions had the breakneck speed of an emotionally charged cross-examination; they were vigorous, like the blood flowing through the veins of a love-crazed person. With the strength of waves crashing against the shore, they lashed the listener with doubt.

'Pyarelal! What are you trying to hint at with all these questions?' For a moment, red smudges of shame appeared in his kohl-lined eyes.

'I'm not trying to suggest anything. I just felt like asking. Do you have any objection answering them?' asked Pyarelal, casting a gaze of suspicion on Amar Singh.

'Now that she is no more, why bring her up unnecessarily?'

The counter-question left Pyarelal agitated. 'What good is our friendship if you keep evading my fair questions?'

'Ah! When it suits you, you invoke bonds of friendship. But how does Hira come between us? Are you friends with me, or was she your true friend?'

Pyarelal offered no answer.

'I've called you to this place to show you something,' Amar Singh said.

'You've changed so quickly as if . . .'

'I am a creature of this world. It's the world that keeps changing.'

'Amar Singh, have I been summoned here to be insulted?'

'I fail to understand what makes you feel slighted?' countered Amar Singh, a sly smile playing on his face. It set Pyarelal ablaze with anger. In great agitation, he uttered a Sanskrit maxim from the Panchatantra, 'Now I can see why they say *vishwastam naati vishwaset*—never blindly trust even the trustworthy.'

'Why do you hurl this wisdom at me? If you look carefully, you'll find its illustration in your own self,' retorted Amar Singh calmly and smiled again.

Pyarelal was red with anger. He got up agitated and said, 'I must leave now. A woman is dead while you sit in her home and ridicule her. Have you no shame? It's only now that I see the true worth of your friendship.'

'Thank you. You've proved yourself to be all talk. Didn't I say the other day that you would eventually forget all about my help and devotion? Once people cease to be useful, the world turns its back on them,' said Amar Singh.

Pyarelal was embarrassed by the riposte. Amar Singh held him by the hand, got him to sit again and looked at his face with imploring eyes. For a while, the room was silent. The names of Hira and Amar Singh kept throbbing in his head, causing a great commotion in his heart. He felt a sudden surge of excitement.

Just then, Pyarelal grabbed Amar Singh by the wrist, but before long—who knows with what all considerations?—released his hold. Today, for the first time, Pyarelal found himself truly appreciating the anguish of a plea.

'Amar Singh, what brings you here? Was Hira known to you?' Pyarelal repeated his questions.

'Yes.'

It was as if someone had wrung Pyarelal's heart dry. 'How come?' he demanded to know.

'Back then she used to live in Kanpur.'

'Where in Kanpur?'

'In Moolganj.'

'What was her profession?' Pyarelal appeared all shaken up, as if trying hard to bring to mind a forgotten fact.

'What profession? She was a student. She had a younger sister too—Shanta. Her father was a rich man, with business interests in Calcutta. When he died, the mother brought the girls to Calcutta. The girls started taking lessons in music and dance. But many were out to ruin their lives, coveting both their beauty and wealth. These were important people, well respected in society. Only the poor among their acquaintants remained loyal to them. Let me summarize this history in brief.

'Her mother died in an accident, and their wealth was all squandered. At the time when she was grappling with a series of misfortunes, the rich laid out their traps to catch her. She guarded her chastity valiantly, but the question of livelihood loomed large. Yet she remained steadfast and tried to make a living through music, like a virtuous woman. Her old maestro, who guided and protected her during days of distress, will testify to her good character. Meanwhile Shanta, her younger sister, kept up her education. She was a student of Bethune College.'

Amar Singh choked up with emotions, and teardrops rolled down his cheeks. Pyarelal was at a complete loss. Why would the story of Shanta make Amar Singh cry?

'If she was a student back then, has she now quit her studies? She must be badly hurt by whatever happened to her sister. Is it possible to meet her?'

'No,' said Amar Singh, wiping his tears. 'I have written a letter to you. Read it once you reach your place, and please pardon my unusual behaviour today.' Saying so, Amar Singh handed Pyarelal a closed envelope. Eager to read the letter, Pyarelal quickly took Amar Singh's leave and opened the envelope much before he reached home.

Pyarelal,

I feel honoured that you love me. The Amar Singh you met here was me. The Amar Singh who used to visit you was Shanta. As she was drawing her last breath, she managed to give out my name and address, meaning she lived here with me. But she didn't get the time to

tell her real name. Having read that news, you would
have suspected foul play and doubted my truth. That's
why, painful though it was, I had to dress up like Amar
Singh. Tomorrow, the newspapers will tell you the
correct story.

Yours,

Hira

Chaturi Chamar[*]

1

Chaturi Chamar is an old resident of Gadhakola—PO Chamiyani, district Unnaon. A little further from my house—built neither by me nor by my father, but by our ancestors—flows a nullah. It gathers water, both filthy and clean, from many sources: from the drains and scuppers in the neighbouring houses; from the occasional rain and the routine household refuse. Chaturi Chamar's ancestral home sits at a corner of a somewhat elevated plot, along the slope of the nullah.

I often wish to pen a paean to him—a common man's life history, or perhaps something of the sort that earned Acharya Mahavir Prasad Dwivedi fulsome praise from Banarasidas Chaturvedi, the famous editor. But there is an issue that makes objectivity a challenge—in the complex web of rural relations, Chaturi happens to be my nephew.

---

[*] Originally published in 1945 in a collection of short stories titled *Chaturi Chamar*.

Chaturi commands immense popularity and respect, since his approach to shoemaking, like the dominant literary trends of the age, is orthodox. His sturdy shoes are admired throughout the countryside. Wearing Chaturi's shoes, the Pasis trap deer, hares and wild pigs, thrice a week; the farmers chase straying cattle away from arhar plants, crushing thorny bushes under their feet; impish boys make their escape from fruit orchards, fenced with prickly climbers, thorny kareel and branches of acacia and wild berries; Dwarka, the barber, walks 2000 miles over two years, handing out ceremonial invitations. But their shoes remain wholly intact and unchanging, as if they were the very embodiment of conservative values.

It is true that Chaturi's shoes are much lighter compared to those from the Banda district. Perhaps, being close to Chritrakoot, our tanner brothers from Banda have inherited the harsh discipline of Lord Ram's penance. And being close to Lucknow, the likes of Chaturi have inherited the easy manners of the nawabs.

During those days, I used to live in my village. Since Chaturi was an immediate neighbour, I didn't have to probe hard to conclude that he was well versed in Bhakti literature; far better, in fact, than most Chaturvedis and other such learned castes. However, unlike the Chaturvedis, he was illiterate. As a result, their outputs were different, even though they laboured alike: Chaturvedis edited books and periodicals, Chaturi 'edited' shoes.

One day, I arranged for some charas and hosted an adda at my own house. Chaturi and others like him were invited. Chaturi was somewhat younger than my uncle. With the help of a few enterprising local boys and the charas-addicted devotees of Ram, a tambourine fitted with bells was also brought in. The soirée started at eight in the evening, with bhajans of Kabirdas, Surdas, Tulsidas, Paltudas and several other saint poets—some known, some unknown—being chorused in quick succession. Until that day, I couldn't appreciate the word *nirgun* beyond its literal meaning: the one with no qualities. When people praised a song calling it a fine nirgun, I would merely chuckle. But now, at the mere mention of the word, my heart overflows with devotion. Perhaps the deluge of advancing age causes the river of wisdom to swell too. And so I sat on a stool and soaked in the music.

Whenever a stanza was missed, Chaturi would pitch in with the missing lines, lecturing like a learned acharya. That day, I also learnt that Chaturi was an authority on Kabir's poetry.

'My dear Kaka, even the greatest of scholars fail to grasp these subtle nirgun couplets,' he said. And then, perhaps counting me among those 'greatest of scholars', he added, 'You see, this couplet suggests . . .'

'Chaturi, for now, why don't you stick only to singing? You can come back tomorrow and do all the explaining you want. Meaning overload will ruin my appetite for music,' I cut in, dismayed at the implied insult.

Chaturi cleared his throat and, turning somewhat serious, resumed his recitation of Kabir couplets.

Between songs, charas was smoked to add gusto to the performance. It was so much fun! Hoping to make the swinging soirée more vibrant, I too clapped to the tunes. I was awestruck by the knowledge the reputedly low-born commanded; they knew full well what those subtle, first-grade songs conveyed. Quite a few of those compositions were dense with metaphors. The songsters understood them too. I sat there till late into the night; little did I know that *bhagat* means nightlong singing. By then, half the charas was already over, and I was quite heavy-eyed. I politely sought Chaturi's permission to leave.

'Kaka, but what will happen to all the fun we're having?' asked Chaturi, drawing attention to the remaining stack of charas with his eyes.

'Chaturi, you know how I live. Your kaki has left for her heavenly abode. I've to cook the meals myself. There is no helping hand around. If I don't rest a little, I may not have the strength to wake up next morning.'

'Only you're to be blamed. You refuse to remarry, or a dozen kakis would've made a beeline for you. But yes, there may not be another like . . .' Chaturi complained, his tone mournful.

'It's all just God's wish,' I defended myself.

'Kaki was such an educated woman. I got her to write many of my letters,' reminisced Chaturi, consoling me with a heavy heart. He then puffed hard at the chillum, inhaled a lungful of charas smoke, pressed his head down firmly, let a white plume waft out of his nostrils and spoke in a choked voice, 'She cooked, she cleaned, she recited the Ramayana daily. She could sing too. And how! Your vocals are no match to hers. I remember your old uncle would sit at the entrance, listening to Kaki recite the Ramayana. Ghazal, tillana and what not—she could croon just about anything. Couldn't she, Kaka?'

'You're right, Chaturi. But you carry on singing. I'll now retire to my house and listen to your songs from behind closed doors,' I said.

2

For as long as I was awake, the bhagat continued unabated; I can't say at what hour of the night it stopped. When I woke up the next morning, the sun was already quite high.

Chaturi was squatting outside, staring unblinkingly at the door. It seems that no one had cared for his insightful gloss on Kabir's *Padawali*. Since I had promised to lend a patient ear in the morning, he was reporting for duty.

'So, Chaturi, did you not get any sleep?' I inquired in jest.

'If I had allowed myself to sleep soundly, it would've been quite late by the time I woke up. I'm here since you had asked me to come,' answered Chaturi, his tone oozing purpose.

Only the truly inspired ones can dare to become unsalaried teachers. 'I'm ready. But first, let me see you explain one of Kabir's *ulatbaasi*—those misleading riddle-like poems.'

'Which one?' Chaturi asked in earnest. 'There are so many good ones, each in its own league. You see, Kaka, I'm a Kabirpanthi, a true disciple of Kabir. Wherever I encounter a knot, Kabir Sahab unties it for me.'

'You're an adept, Chaturi. I realized that last night.'

Chaturi closed his eyes, as if lost in a deep reverie contemplating Kabir Sahab. He then began intoning a Kabir poem, explaining each line as he sang. Were I to interrupt that rhapsodic rendition, it would have spoilt all the fun.

I waited till he was done singing and discoursing. Once he stopped—having impressed me the way the 'vegetarian' articles of *Kalyan* magazine impress the Hindiwallahs—I remarked, 'Chaturi, if only you were literate, you would have landed a job worth five hundred rupees a month.'

Chaturi was elated. 'Kaka, if it agrees with you, shall I ask Arjunwa to come to you for studies? If you take him under your wing, he'll become literate, absorb some of your knowledge. I'll also teach him all I know. God willing, he'll make something of his life. What do you say?'

'Do send him. Also, tell him to bring along a diya. There's only one lantern in my house. I fear if he comes too frequently, the villagers may find it shocking and frown upon us, but we'll see about that later. And yes, I'll charge a tuition fee on a daily basis. But don't worry. He just needs to fetch me meat from the market and, twice a month, take wheat to the flour mill. He'll be paid for his work. Besides, you too go frequently to the market.'

Chaturi was elated by the terms of engagement. Presently, I steered the conversation to a context I was eager to broach and said, 'Chaturi, your shoes draw such fulsome praise.'

Pleased at the praise, Chaturi replied, 'Yes, Kaka, they last two full years.' But in that emphatic assertion, I could also read latent agony. 'Kaka, every year, I'm made to give away a pair to the zamindar's strongman. Bhagatwa and Panchma offer a pair each too. When my own shoes last for two years, why would someone hanker for more and waste precious leather?'

As Chaturi stated his simple quandary, he appeared to be overcome with grief, his eyes brimming over with tears. I felt a surge of empathy tinged with laughter coming on, but I remained tight-lipped. Once he appeared somewhat composed, I spoke to him lovingly. 'Chaturi, we'll have to look it up in the Wazib-ul-Arz, the record of customs. If the annual tribute of a shoe is mentioned in it, you'll have to keep up the practice—down through the generations.'

Chaturi reflected on the possibility and smiled. 'What do you think, Kaka? Is this mentioned in the Abdul-Arj?' asked Chaturi, mispronouncing the name of the document.

'Hmmm, you should try to find it out. It'll cost only a rupee,' I replied.

Since it was already quite late and I had some work, I saw him off. As he walked away solemnly, twitching his head, I tried reading his dilemma. 'He is trapped in a vicious net he is desperate to tear himself free from. He feels himself up to the task, musters up all his strength, but a single weakness causes him endless frustration.'

3

Arjun started coming to me for his studies. Those days, I had little engagement outside the *dehat*, the deep countryside, and stayed mostly at home. There was an uninterrupted supply of fresh meat. Every now and then, I threw a *brahma bhoj*, a sacramental feast, to which the Loghs, Pasis, Dhobis and Chamars were invited. Whoever salivated at the smell of ghee-roasted, spicy meat, petitioned me to invite him to the banquets. Come to think of it, my house had become a veritable adda of ordinary people—the House of Commons.

Meanwhile, Arjun made visible progress in his studies. Initially, when he learnt to spell the names of relations—Dada, Mama, Kaka, Didi, Nani, etc.—his parents, overjoyed, roamed the village, displaying the proud bearings of a royalty. People gossiped that Arjun had learnt all about complex blood relations, that he was now well-read in Dada-Didi. Arjun addressed his father as Dada and mother as Didi. Once, his elder brother approached me with a complaint. 'Baba, Arjun can write all the words in the world, yet he never spells Bhaiya.' I had to explain that the books lavish greater importance on parents than on an elder brother; it would take Arjun two months by the time he reached the word 'Bhaiya.'

Gradually, it was that time of the year when mangoes ripened. By then, Arjun, having finished a second book on the Hindi language, had earned great distinction throughout his clan. Perhaps he had grown a tad delicate, too; he now had difficulty doing hard labour.

Meanwhile, I went to my in-laws to fetch my son; I wanted my dear boy to relish the season of fresh mangoes. Back then, he must've been nine or ten—perhaps a student in the fourth grade.

At my ancestral home, there was nothing to keep him entertained. Not even a woman to pamper him with motherly affection. But the lad wasn't bored. Within a few days, he seemed to have developed a deep bond of friendship with Arjun. If I was like a father to Arjun, my son had become a veritable uncle. Even though Arjun was nearly twice his age, yet, in terms of social status and education, the little 'Uncle' was his superior. He was a Brahmin's son, after all.

Given Arjun's youthful age, lavishing reverence on his new guardian—a much younger kaka—required belittling his own true self; it felt unnatural. Within a few days, the humiliating ordeal took a heavy toll on his health.

I had no clue as to what had transpired between them while I was away; Arjun wasn't in the habit of complaining. Whenever I returned home, either from the post office or from a trip to another village, I found my son toiling hard at tutoring Arjun. He would be closely supervising his disciple's progress, sometimes at Arjun's home, sometimes at my own place.

As Tulsidas observes in the *Ramcharitmanas*, 'It is with great excitement that a lion's cub stalks a herd of crazed elephants.' In the colony of the Chamars, I've seen this maxim come to life, time and again. It was plain to me that my son's urge to dominate and torment Arjun drew its strength from his Brahminical values. I wanted to lecture him. But what change could my sermon have brought? Brahmins will oppress the Chamars, and the latter will submit to the oppression—such has been the regrettable way of the world. Yes, this malady can be cured if the roots the castes sprout from are torn up. But it's easier said than done. And so I kept mum.

Whenever I taught Arjun, my demeanour was affectionate. I always respected him as a fellow human; I looked past the errors in his pronunciation. The open fissures of his flaws would get fixed in the near future, or so I told myself. Not once did I bother to keep an account of his mistakes. But within that short period of time, my son had identified all of Arjun's shortcomings. On the pretext of tutoring, he would summon Arjun home—whenever he felt like it, regardless of time—and amuse himself as the latter struggled to pronounce words properly. All this went on in my absence. I learnt of this only later.

It was a Monday, the day of the weekly market in Mianganj. I had already given money to Chaturi to buy meat. Those days, the post office was in Magrayar, not too far from Mianganj. I decided to amble towards the weekly market, carrying postage stamps for the dispatches. Chaturi was busy at his kiosk. I approached him and said, 'Kalika Bhaiya, the washerman, is also here in the market. Please ask him to carry along my supply of meat. You'll be busy till the market lasts. It will get quite late.'

'Kaka, there's something I need to talk to you about. Since Arjunwa is scared of you, he won't do it himself. When I come to your place, I'll explain it all. Please don't be offended. It's a juvenile matter, concerning the two boys,' Chaturi humbly submitted.

'All right' was all I could say at the time, but I imagined many possibilities. I greeted the butcher and sauntered away towards the Baniyas for almond thandai.

Those who knew my habits well were busily introducing my virtues to those who didn't; I was the subject of general gossip in the market, hounded all around by probing eyes. People were shocked that if I was indeed what I was, how come I had taken to the most loathsome sin of meat-eating. I had grown quite accustomed to such situations; within seconds, I could read it all in their eyes. The ordained Brahmins had stopped dining with me. Local boys had done well to turn their God-fearing parents and grandparents against me. 'He brags I'm no "Pani Pandey" dying to offer water to all and sundry,' the boys said, quoting me falsely.

This added fuel to the fire. Just as I was 'famous' in the literary circuits, my 'reputation' reached all the remote nooks of social circuits too. Particularly since the day I had parlayed with the Swamiji who had lavished fulsome 'praise' on the chapatti parties organized at the village school.

I told Swamiji the tale of a kebab-eating sage who lived in Kabul during the days of Ramachandra, disseminating Indian wisdom in that distant land. My story left him so dumbfounded that even though I was smoking a bidi, that too in the midst of the village Brahmins, he could not bring himself to condemn me. Luckily, that day, my wastrel of a servant was carrying a bidi. As I puffed hard at the borrowed bidi, I sent out a clear message to Swamiji: to me, you are as worthless as the smoke I am spouting.

Reeling under the prickly gaze of the marketplace that dripped with shock and scorn, I finished my glass of almond thandai. But just as I was trying to straighten my strained spine, I spotted an elderly panditji walking towards me. He was accompanied by a village rustic. 'Here comes another sermon!' I thought to myself. But I was in for a surprise. Panditji eschewed all the complaints, put on a pleased countenance and asked his companion in a honeyed tone, 'Is he that gentleman?'

'Yes, he is the one,' answered the rustic.

Panditji appeared elated at seeing me. He raised his chin, looked up and said, 'Ah, you are a blessed soul.'

'No, I'm a wild soul. The old wretch is trying to scorch me with sarcasm,' I thought to myself. I looked closely at his turban and walking stick, and said, 'I offer my pranam, Panditji.'

Overcome with affection, Panditji was at a loss for words. My pranam is no ordinary salutation; only the very fortunate receive it. As I stood there watching Panditji, the latter turned to his companion and asked again, 'Has the gentleman cleared all the academic exams? *Beeye, Meeye* ... everything?'[*]

His companion solemnly replied, 'Yes, not one person in the entire district can match his education.'

Biting my lips, I said, 'Panditji, there are two canals and a river on the way to my home. What's more, the road is infested with wolves too. And I haven't brought my lathi. If I have your permission, I'd like to set out for home—it's getting dark.'

Panditji stared at me lovingly. He had heard all about me, all the usual complaints. But now, having met me, his eyes seemed to cast doubt on all that censure. His gaze bared his heart. 'He is nothing like what they say. He surely doesn't eat meat, nor does he smoke. People are nasty.' I bowed to him, sought his blessings and took the path leading home.

As I reached my place, I stopped at the door; I could hear voices coming from inside.

'Speak, you loser, speak up,' it was my son's voice. I could gather the import of that domineering note—that *veer* rasa his voice exuded. Arjun had given up trying to correct his pronunciation. However, my good son, thoroughly relishing Arjun's discomfiture, was far from tired. He kept ordering him to say the words. Being compelled to repeat himself, Arjun had grown bored of the drill. But when my son scolded him again, Arjun reluctantly muttered, 'What word?'

---

[*] Panditji, supposedly a learned man, struggles to pronounce 'BA' and 'MA'.

'That same word: guña. Say it.'

'Gooda,' Arjun repeated. The room echoed with the boy's derisive guffaw. Once he had laughed to his heart's content, he composed himself and issued a fresh command. '"Now say Ganesh.'

'Gades,' whimpered Arjun. Another burst of laughter ensued, at the end of which Arjun was brutally reproached. 'Gades-fades . . . what rubbish! Why can't you speak clearly for once? Tell me, moron, don't you clean your tongue daily with a twig?'

Dumbfounded by the terrible insult, Arjun could only let out a lifeless mumble, his head bowed in shame. I had set the door ajar and was observing everything from behind a pillar. My son glowered at him with the same castigating gaze White folks cast on the Blacks. After a brief pause, he hurled another command, 'Now say "varna".'

Arjun grew pale with panic. Sensing his painful predicament, I felt both amused and angry. It was clear to me this Arjun here couldn't have wielded the mighty bow of knowledge. Trying to spell varna, he was all worn out. Even though Arjun made all manners of sorry faces, he couldn't vocalize his quandary. Taking delight in the intense despondence that disfigured Arjun's face, my brave son issued a fresh, violent rebuke. 'Will you speak up or do you want me to slap you hard across your face? So what if your touch pollutes me? I'll take a shower. It's hot anyway.'

I thought it was about time I announced my presence. As soon as Arjun saw me, he sprang to his feet and burst into tears, wiping his eyes with both hands. I turned to my 'gem of a son' and ordered, 'Grab your ears and do ten sit-ups.'

'I haven't done anything. Why should I be punished?' protested my son, taking care to avoid my gaze.

'You've shown him utter disrespect,' I countered.

'You, too, must've treated him this way. Just get him to say "guna". You must've taught him that word too. It's here in his book.'

'But why were you laughing at him?' I demanded.

'I didn't make fun of him on purpose.'

'Well, from this day, you're not allowed to speak to him.'

'Fine, just send me back to my Mamaji's place. The mangoes here are too sour. Besides, when I pluck them off the branches, their sap burns my mouth. Back there they taste much sweeter as they're plucked raw and set to ripen in baskets.'

I sent him away, escorted by a local barber, hoping that this would offer some consolation to Chaturi and Arjun.

4

I had to stay at the village for a few more months. During this period, Arjun made sure to add to his stock of learning. I hadn't seen the city lights for a long time. Travelling through Calcutta, Banaras and Prayag, I finally reached Lucknow, mainly to see to the publication of my previously accepted manuscripts. However, I ended up being heaped with new writing assignments. I rented a room at a hotel in Ameenabad and prepared for literary pursuits, my mind completely at ease.

Those were the heady days of revolution shaking the country—the one ignited by Chaturi and the likes. My young city friends, newly retuned from dehat, told me how Gadhakola, too, was on the boil. The farmers had declared a strike after tilling through 600–700 bighas; that land now lay fallow, with none left to sow it. I was also told that the protesting farmers got together every day to sing the *jhanda geet*, the revolutionary song of the flag. A year later, the revolution elicited a sharp reaction from the adversary; the zamindar struck back through false debt claims and oppressed the tenants without mercy.

Driven to the wall, the village leader visited me with an anxious plea: 'Come with us to the village, stay there and do all the writing you want. With you around, we'll be spared the thrashing. It will give us strength and courage. Of late, the tyranny has been much too brutal.'

'I'm no policeman. How am I supposed to protect you? Besides, I lack the patience to suffer in silence. What if I react violently if assaulted?' I tried to reason with them.

'You don't have to get involved. Just stay with us,' the village headman assured me. So I went with them.

The village Congress committee had strange ways—it had no contacts with the district unit, nor did it maintain a register of members. But when it came to action programmes, no village in the Poorva division could match its record. While I was away, the zamindar had fallen into the habit of submitting pleas and complaints—God knows how many and to whom all.

A tricolour flag—coloured with raw dyes and hoisted atop a bamboo pole—was planted right across the Mahavir Swami temple. But the rains had washed it white.

During those days, lawsuits were launched thick and fast, and police investigations were rigorous. The local landlord had filed a lawsuit against a few farmers, falsely projecting one year's outstanding tribute as three years' default. Moreover, buoyed by his innate pettiness, he had also approached the honorary magistrate with his complaint. This had made matters worse. The zamindar's good reputation among the farmers stood damaged beyond repair; to them, he had become a veritable monster.

One day—perhaps compelled by the mounting pile of documents and complaint letters—the daroga came to investigate the matter. I was planning to go to the Magrayar post office. As soon as I hit the road, the villagers surrounded me. 'Darogaji has come, please stay back for now.' Before long I met the daroga too. The landlord pointed at me and said something quietly to him in English. Since I was a bit distant from them, I couldn't gather what had passed between the two. The villagers, too, couldn't follow the exchange. The daroga was now walking towards the flag. The landlord seemed intent on getting it removed. The sight of a flag in the temple courtyard set the daroga thinking. 'This is a temple flag,' he inferred. He examined it closely; there was no colour visible on it. And then he turned his gaze to the zamindar and started walking back towards the camp.

The zamindar tried his best to convince the daroga that it was a Congress flag washed clean by the rain. But the daroga was a clever man. He refused to order the removal of the flag merely to flex the proverbial administrative muscle. Besides, the existence of a Congress committee in the village could not be verified—neither by the divisional committee nor by the district committee. What was the poor daroga supposed to do?

Those days, since I was afflicted with insomnia, my head was tonsured. Moreover, I had put on the demeanour of a village rustic. 'So what if I lack the looks? I must compensate with good communication, otherwise the thanedar will have a very poor opinion of me. Just as Mahavir's blessings had saved the flag, I, too, must invoke Saraswati's grace to wriggle out of this situation.' As I was juggling these thoughts, the thanedar shot a question at me, 'Are you with the Congress?'

It was clear to me that under the circumstances, measured bureaucratic language would serve greater purpose than the exuberance of Hindi. 'Well, I belong to the congress of the world,' I answered.

But the thanedar did not get the drift. 'What Congress is this?' he demanded to know.

Ambushed with that unexpected question, a thought crossed my mind: If I'm to become a sentinel of truth, like Yudhisthira, I will be pardoned the sin of lying. 'The people of this village don't even know what congress means,' I stated the truth. However, I knew that if that conversation stretched any longer, I could soon land in trouble. So I decided to make my escape. 'All right then, I will get going now,' I said, adding, 'I've got some business at the post office. The postman comes this way only twice a week, bringing me important letters, registered posts, newspapers, periodicals and such. Besides, we also have a library in the village. I need to visit it too.'

'Does Congress send you letters?' bluntly inquired the daroga.

'No, I get only personal letters.'

The thanedar left, perhaps a little upset with the zamindar.

The investigation had warded off immediate troubles, but the lawsuit continued. The honorary magistrate, who was a relative of the zamindar's lawyer, passed a verdict validating the zamindar's claims over the farmers. Chaturi's interventions in the matter came much later.

An appeal was filed against the verdict. But, by then, the funds pooled in for the collective defence had been already exhausted. During the first case itself, many were forced to auction off their cattle and other assets. Total panic had set in. Chaturi harboured no hope for help; the villagers did not contribute again for Chaturi and others.

One day, Chaturi came and stood before me, drained and helpless. 'Chaturi, I will do everything in my power to help you.' I tried to console him with words of assurance.

'To what extent will you help, Kaka?' There was a clear ring of despondency to Chaturi's voice, as if he were a helpless man slowly drowning in a well.

'What is your plan?' I asked, my eyes fixed on him.

'I will fight the case. But the villagers are scared, and they won't testify against the zamindar,' Chaturi replied with a heavy heart. I, too, felt saddened by the situation.

'What now, Chaturi?' I asked, my tone still anxious.

Chaturi replied, 'Well, what more can I say? Let the zamindar gobble up all the sweets.'

5

I arranged for a few reliable witnesses in the village. Chaturi walked ten kilometres to Unnao, carrying a bag of sattu to eat; he did not take the train. After the second deposition, he walked back wearing a radiant smile on his face and announced, 'Kaka, I know it now: the annual tribute of a pair of shoes is not mentioned in the Abdul-Arj.'

Devi[*]

1

For twelve years on the trot, I kept fiddling around, weaving worthless webs of words. To my mind, I was building a *chakravyooh*—an impenetrable labyrinth—for the defence of literature. Such an enterprise, I had sincerely hoped, would not only yield beautiful works of art but would also help me control the unbridled fervour of the literary imagination. Sadly, it wasn't meant to be; people feared getting lost in my chakravyooh, and the end result was quite the opposite of what was intended by my original design. Whenever I spoke of a literary heaven, people's thoughts turned to their own death and afterlife; this was a sad misreading of my words. Now I see why I never garnered much respect, and why I suffered such privation. But even during my days of heady penury, I harboured luxuriant dreams of fairies. Sadly, the more

---

[*] Published in the anthology *Chaturi Chamar*, 1945.

I tried to uplift society through my writings, the harder it tried to pull me down. And since I was on a mission to create a literary heaven, rescuing literature from hellfire, my own world kept drifting away. Now that I've switched to another realm, that old world appears to me like a corpse lying in the distance.

Studying my ravenous friends, eager to reap profits from others' losses, I realized the true meaning of a popular maxim: 'A delicacy draws Brahmins; a cremation ground attracts dogs.' Loafers to start with, but now magnates! My friends have built double-storey houses and drive expensive cars. They throw such patronizing looks at me, as though I were their servant. I've also heard them murmur: 'He is a good man all right, but a bit crazy.' And then the entire coterie dissolves into laughter. They have become big and important, and moved ahead of me, while I'm still trudging wearily along the same old road.

Perhaps I ought to bid farewell to poetry before my days come to an end. This cursed art has brought me nothing but infamy; it nearly had my name fade into oblivion and robbed me of the little worth that I possessed. Perhaps not writing what people consider nuisance would be the keenest way to appreciate what our society truly appreciates. Besides, it doesn't take much to master the art of writing popular books of titillation, such as *Rati Shastra*, *Vanita-Vinod*, *Kam Kalyan*. I can always produce books like these, gleaning readily the essence of four others of this ilk. And as for writing pious accounts of Sita, Savitri and Damayanti, I can scribble one of those even with my eyes shut. If I make these little adjustments, no one would find anything offensive about me. Not even those who inflict biographies of virtuous women on their wives, even as they delve deep into treatises on the *chaurasi aasan*, or the eighty-four sex positions, albeit in secrecy. You see, it was only in my bid to tarnish Indian culture that I ended up tarnishing myself. But hereafter, I promise to mend my ways.

Let us first understand that Ram, Shyam and all such figures who command our veneration—deities and 'distinguished' *bhakts* alike—were no ordinary persons. Each of them enjoyed eminence. And acclaim doesn't come without eminence. One can't become distinguished as a *rajrshi*, a royal sage, without first being a raja; or legendary as a *brahmarshi* without first being a Brahmin. No one has heard of a *vaisyarshi* or a *shudrarshi*—neither in history books nor in scriptures.[*] Put plainly, this is simply impossible. The point is, eminence by birth is a prerequisite for a respectable life. A big kingdom, great wealth, huge ships, railways, telegraph, cannons and gunpowder, guns and bullets, warships, torpedoes, mines, submarines, chemical weapons, troops and police, palaces and gardens—these don't fit into a man's normal field of vision for a good reason. Their colossal size is meant to keep the small people mindful of their smallness. From Chandra, Surya, Varun, Kubera, Yama, Jayant, Indra, Brahma, Vishnu and Mahesh, all the way up to the Supreme God—even the realm of gods is ordered according to a similar hierarchy.

Lounging in a recliner chair laid out on the hotel veranda, I grappled with these thoughts, trying to review my own fate in their light. Since the aforementioned

---

[*] The suffix *rshi* means a sage or a sage-like person. Nirala ridicules its affected exclusivity, which debars all except Brahmins and kings from being sage-like.

was an impromptu tirade, there may have been some
thoughtlessness in its content; discerning readers would
read carefully. But the mere thought of being an eminent
person set my veins taut with a rush of blood. Buoyed by
the miraculous word 'eminent', I straightened my arched
spine and sat upright, looking all enthused.

I threw a haughty glance at the road, as if I was
an eminent person already, my little inadequacies
notwithstanding. My eyes fell on a woman. She was sitting
by the road, wrapped in a tattered sari, her hair cropped.
The woman observed every passer-by with her curious
gaze. Her face was smeared dark with dirt, and her breasts
dangled bare. I felt overcome with a sudden surge of
emotions; 'What on earth is this?' the voice within echoed.
She was not even twenty-five, braving the blows of nature
all by herself, withering away under an open sky. Perhaps
others may have found her to be somewhat older. A baby
boy—about eighteen months of age—played next to her.
There was nothing conventionally feminine about her. The
moment I caught sight of her, my smugness evaporated
before her pitiable being, and the feeling of smallness took
hold of me all over again. I started worrying about her.
'Who is she? A Hindu or a Muslim? She also has a child to
support. What does the future hold for these two? Will the
child be raised and educated by the roadside? What does
the woman think of God, society, religion and humanity?'

As I sat plagued by these questions, I summoned the
hotel attendant. His name was Sangamlal, but I jestingly
called him Sang Malal, or the one tailed by grudges. When
he appeared before me, I inquired after that woman.
Sangamlal smiled at me and said, 'Babu, she is a *pagli*, a

mad woman, and a mute too. We feed her leftovers from our guests' plates.' He finished explaining with a laugh and returned to his chores, making light of the matter.

My sense of eminence stood humbled by the sight of this woman; for all my greatness, I brought her no hope. I knew her fate could not be turned around. The cycle of joys and sorrows, as described by astrologers, had come to a halt in her life. Having suffered unending hardship, she must have grown numb to sorrows. I imagined her sitting under a shady tree, or on a deserted veranda, weathering heat waves, sometimes casting an impassive glance at the blazing noon sky. Perhaps her child's innocent laughter brought her some comfort on such dreary days. Nobody can tell how many rainy days, winters or summers she had survived in the open. People heap adulation on the exploits of Napoleon, but whoever spares a thought for this woman's fortitude? Everyone calls her 'Pagli', but aren't those very people responsible for her degrading transformation? What endowments make a man great, or what deprivation leads to his undoing—who can explain these mysterious things? Did Pagli also grow up by the roadside, like her child? It's likely that at first she was only a mute but was banished from home after her marriage. Or maybe she ran away herself, trying to escape the torture inflicted on her by her in-laws, and the child was fathered by someone she had met on the streets.

The sprite that lived deep in her heart, hidden like a flame shrouded in smoke, wanted to fly away from this world. The woman's complexion was dark. In fact, there was nothing about her that would've appeared pleasing to the world. Naturally, some treated her badly, while others avoided looking her way. But as for me, I saw a person

I wanted to bring to life in literature with my imagination, not just her shape but her soul too. Not even the greatest of poets would've fathomed her voiceless majesty, or pictured a form and bearing so exceptional as hers. I had read a lot about emotions and speech patterns. In books of philosophy, I had also come across studies about the subtle recesses of the human mind. I had seen Rabindranath act on stage and had tried my own hand at writing. I had even known those who could miraculously produce animal and bird sounds to summon them. But while they were all artificial, everything about Pagli seemed real. How do I put into words those subtle gestures the mother–son pair communicated with? The poor mute was trying to teach her child the voiceless language she spoke. The child, too, never called out to its mother; it spoke to her merely with its eyes. Could anyone guess what it wanted to convey? Well, the mother could. Would you still consider her *pagli* and mute?

2

Those days, I busied myself studying Pagli; she became my greatest source of wisdom. Whenever I saw her I was reminded of Mahashakti, the great feminine power. Could there be a clearer manifestation of Mahashakti? Nothing could have taught me more about the world than Pagli. She was like a resplendent morning whose first light woke me up, washing away the utopian dreams of Ram, Krishna and other divine souls. Faced with the reality of Pagli, the greatest of civilizations and the grandest centres of learning found themselves pummeled to dust. That Mahashakti took possession of my mind, its might firmly entrenched. I saw the truest image of Bharat mirrored in her child. And as for Pagli, well, what can I say?

There are many big universities in the country that charge a hefty fee for education. I wonder what fate awaits this child. Will it ever get educated? And he has a mother too. What portion of the nation's sympathy will fall to her share? Is she entitled to more than the leftover chapatis on our plates that previously went to the dogs? To me, Pagli and her son represented the real portrait of our society. Sitting by the road with a baby by her side, the mute mother imparted lessons on religion, science, politics, society and all such subjects dear to mankind. But who could really gather her teachings? This world's essence lies in its dogged refusal to acknowledge the truth. This is what Pagli appeared to suggest over and over again. Her soul rang out a poignant cry: Society may have denied her both space and empathy, but is she any less human than others? She, too, has a child to rear.

One day, I saw a political leader's procession pass through the same road. Thousands marched together, rending the air with slogans and ovations. I stood on the veranda, marvelling at the rousing welcome the leader was being treated to. Even Pagli rose to her feet and looked at the scene with wonder. Perhaps she had never seen a crowd so large on her road. She was trying hard to make sense of the experience, her mouth agape, eyes widened and brows drawn together for focus. Can the reader guess how much of it she could understand? Just then, her child got trampled upon by someone in the crowd and let out a loud wail. Agitated, Pagli tried to comfort it with warm kisses, wiping the dust off its little body. She then turned her angry gaze to the crowd, her eyes raining fire. Well, this is all I could gather from the scene. Meanwhile, the leader walked away with the bag carrying the money he had raised during the rally—Rs 10,000, to be spent on the welfare of the poor and other important causes.

Sometime later, the Ramayani Samaj organized an event, not too far from where Pagli usually sat. It was a Sunday, and a huge contingent of bhakts had turned up for the devotional gathering. The ritual recitation of Goswami Tulsidas's *Ramcharitmanas* commenced at two o'clock and concluded by five. Through his epic, as is well known to readers, Goswami Tulsidas has added a further touch of purity to the already purified Hindu comportment. After relishing the recitation, the purified devotees dispersed. On their way back, many took notice of Pagli, squatting with her child—poor, emaciated and shorn of the slightest trace of eminence. A man said, 'See for yourself: both heaven and hell exist in this very world.' Another said, 'She is paying for her bad karma.' A third quoted Tulsidas to brand Paglia wastrel: 'The world has everything a man may desire but nothing for the one who fails to strive.' For the fast-thinning crowd, Pagli became an excuse to indulge in scholastic discourses and debate destiny.

'Babu, she is a Muslim,' Sangamlal reported one day. When I asked him how he knew that, I was told that people said so. 'She was born a Hindu but later became a Muslim. In fact, it was a Muslim who fathered her child. Earlier, she was neither mad nor mute; the ailments afflicted her later,' Sangamlal narrated with interest.

I heard him out patiently, trying to guess why he shared the story with me. Those days, I discussed Pagli's case with many. Her story prompted debates on the ideals of literature, politics and other such hallowed subjects. Some laughed, while others left looking solemn. A few gave money to relieve Pagli's distress.

Hindus, Muslims, high-ranking officials, kings and patricians—I've seen them all cast passing glances at Pagli as they ambled down that road. But I haven't noticed a single look of concern or sympathy. Those too absorbed in themselves can never establish emotional links with others; their eyes penetrate no deeper than the cold exterior of another person. I knew this all too well. Considering a living person as dead, and a dead one as alive, is both a delusion and a form of knowledge. Deer and foxes take a scarecrow to be a living person, while the wise squirrels scamper about living bodies thinking they are carved in stone. To what category was Pagli consigned by her superiors? Living or dead? Only God knows!

One day, a police parade was held in the city. Pagli watched the event sitting on the sidewalk, while I looked on from the veranda, my torso naked. My appearance was the subject of general amusement; quite a few sepoys smiled at me. My long, flowing hair and my face provoked many into calling me 'Miss Fashion'. Each time I walked into a theatre or a cinema, the moniker was repeatedly hurled at me. Some teased me even on the roads. I could see that the sepoys, too, were tickled by the 'Miss Fashion' look I flaunted. But I always refrained from reacting to the jeers. Deep down I knew that under the circumstances, a haircut was the best rejoinder. Besides, if I had retorted, my window into other people's mind would have been shut.

Sometimes I wondered if the hecklers ever thought about the world of pain that awaited them, were I to smack them hard. But that's okay. It was clear to me that none feared me; my chiselled Greek physique, nearly six-foot-tall frame, unusually broad shoulders and toned muscles did not intimidate anyone. And so I stopped worrying about the prying eyes and turned my gaze towards Pagli. As always, she was sitting quietly by the road. The sepoys marched with military precision—left-right, left-right—causing the earth to tremble with their proud gait. But Pagli was strangely amused; she kept laughing at them. And the more she laughed, the angrier the white sepoys got. She troubled the British on our behalf, I was happy to imagine. She even tried to draw her child into the fun. A mother always ensures the best for her child—the noblest of lessons, the finest of things. She kept snapping her fingers at the boy, and with the other hand, pointed repeatedly at the parading sepoys, as if asking in great mirth: 'Aren't you also amused? What a fun sight it is, eh?'

Many months passed by. Owing to our daily interactions, Pagli and I came to know each other quite well. In fact, to her, I was a veritable bodyguard. The local boys used to tease her all the time. If I happened to be around, she would pull a sad face and turn to me for support, pointing at the leering boys. Seeing me, the hoodlums would leave her be. Gradually, our intimacy deepened, and she began seeing me as her greatest benefactor. I used to give her money and would often persuade my friends to do the same. I know she could understand all that. One day, I learnt that some thugs were routinely stealing her money at night. But there was nothing disquieting about thievery—it is like a religion humans the world over recognize and follow. And so I decided against doing anything about the matter. Besides, Pagli herself seemed eager to put it out of her mind. Since these incidents took place in the dark and she couldn't recognize the culprits, she simply shed some tears and consoled herself.

One day, a friend of mine tried to prank Pagli. Someone had told him that she had amassed massive wealth that lay buried somewhere. To confirm the rumour, he approached her smilingly and, after explaining to her how moneylending works, demanded a loan of two rupees. When Pagli heard his words, she burst into a hearty laugh and, without any hesitation whatsoever, took out the three paise she had tucked at her waist.

3

Pagli and her child withstood another season of scorching summer and heavy rains, while the people of means continued being mere spectators. Whenever it rained, Pagli took refuge on the veranda of an abandoned house. But by the time she collected her belongings and made for the shelter, both she and her bedding would be soaked. Thereafter, she would stay drenched for several hours. Bearing such brutal hardships, her health started showing signs of deterioration.

While she could perform penance and observe the severest of austerities, working for a living was not her forte.

Owing to years of inactivity, her hands and feet had stiffened. There was a faucet by the roadside. To quench her thirst, Pagli had only to saunter across to it. Yet, it took her nearly half an hour to cover the short distance. And if she ever happened to spot a tonga, even if it was one-furlong away, she would not move till it had passed. While an average person would have crossed the road four times over in the span, Pagli would freeze. At times, another ekka would appear in sight soon after the first had left, forcing Pagli to give up on crossing the road after a few spirited attempts. One could tell from her dithering that she feared being run down by a vehicle. On such occasions, her countenance betrayed the tedium she felt, so clearly that anyone could have guessed that she was peeved. 'Is the road meant only for those with motors and tongas? I stop when I see them. Why can't they stop for me?' Thus it would be quite some time before Pagli got the chance to reach the faucet. The readers can imagine how raging her thirst must be by then.

One day, after dinner, we were playing Black Queen, a card game. Since it had rained in the evening, Pagli had moved to the veranda of that empty house. It was ten o'clock in the night. Our hotel's gate was lit up bright. Tables and chairs were neatly arranged along the sidewalk. Having put her child to sleep, Pagli had gone out somewhere. The child lay deep in slumber. But just when it changed position, it slid off the veranda—nearly two feet in height—and fell to the pavement below, letting out a loud scream as it hit the hard surface. My fellow players wasted no time in lashing out at the mother. 'It seems Pagli isn't there,' someone observed. A large-hearted boarder summoned Sangamlal and instructed, 'Go and look for Pagli. Fetch her if she's around.'

These exchanges were laced with a stoic indifference, which whipped me into action. I ran to the wailing child and picked it up. A friend objected, 'Arre, it is dirty.' But I cuddled it in my lap and started rocking it gently. The poor child, which had suffered such a painful fall, stopped crying in no time; it had never known such comfort before. Perhaps its mother didn't know how to rock a child. Even if she did, she might not have had the strength to cradle it. It is true that a child finds greater warmth in a tender lap than from a pair of eyes showering distant adoration. This child was accustomed to injuries and hurts, but perhaps not even once had it basked in such loving care. That is why it forgot its pain and soon drifted into sleep, lying peacefully in my lap, its own cradle of happiness. I carefully returned it to its bed on the veranda.

The winter had slowly started setting in. One day, my friend Mr Naitharni came to me and said, 'The other night, when Pagli's son had fallen off the veranda, you cuddled it in your lap. Dewan Sahib was up at the time. He woke me up, too, so I could also bear witness.'

'I didn't think much of my gesture. According to the Jatakas, the Buddha was prepared to lay down his life for a billy goat. Once we truly become capable of greatness, we'll realize how very ordinary my actions that evening were. But the prevailing trend seems to be all wrong: the one deserving of veneration is rarely worshipped, while those who take to glorifying something shallow become the subject of worship themselves,' I thought to myself.

Some weeks passed. By now, the winter was already quite severe. One day, around midnight, I heard a puppy whining on the street. Having finished writing a story, I was getting ready to go to bed. Others at the hotel were already fast asleep. I stayed in a room on the ground floor, not too far from the street. The hotel's gate was closed. But I opened my room's door nonetheless and stepped out to check on the poor animal. And what did I see? It was Pagli. She was lying on the sidewalk, holding her child, wrapped in a tattered black blanket she must've found somewhere. When Pagli became aware of the cruel world and of her own burdensome existence in it, when the bitter winter pierced her bones and caused her frail body to quiver, she made that mournful noise. Like a whining puppy. A worn-out bedding—stitched together with discarded clothes and drenched in dew—was spread on the road. 'Has God created me only to be a mute onlooker?' I asked myself. My own quilt was so thin that I could not dare sleep in the open. And as for my old garments, the helps at the hotel were quick to claim them. Mathura had taken my kurta, which fitted him like a knee-length achkan. He wore it at night, having altered the length of its arms. Sangamlal had layered my dhoti with his and was using it to keep himself warm. Maharaja, the cook, had tied a rakhi around my wrist and demanded a blanket in return for his affection, which I was yet to deliver. Who could have given that old blanket to Pagli, I wondered. Just then I was reminded of the generous women from a rich Bengali family that lived across the road. Every now and then, they gave Pagli a sari and dressed her child in old and discarded English frocks. They must have donated the blanket too. Thinking these thoughts, tears welled up in my eyes.

One day, livid with the hotel's proprietor, nearly a dozen boarders got together and decided to leave as a group. They were all students and quite fond of me. Some of them studied at Canning College, while the others were enrolled at Christian College. The two boys leading the rebels, both students of law, approached me and spoke in confidence. 'Janaab, it's not feasible that we deposit a month's rent here and then go find another place to live, with money enough for both advance rent and other needs. We will certainly clear our dues at this place, but only bit by bit. The money we get from home barely covers a month's expenses. We will ask for more, and once we get it, we'll pay the proprietor. The manager has been telling us that this hotel will soon be pulled down. If that happens before the month's end, where will we go? Our exams are just around the corner. Therefore, we've already made the necessary arrangements.'

My thoughts turned to Pagli. Soon, there would be no leftovers for her to survive on. And now that she was too frail to walk around, she couldn't have found another place where she could sit and beg. Meanwhile, the students left with the resolve (and it was only now that I got it) that they would exact revenge for all the unsavoury meals served to them by making the hotel's proprietor run around to collect his dues.

Once the students left, the hotel wore a deserted look. It was decided that the place would be shut down by the end of the month. Sangamlal came to me one morning, dressed in a vest I had given him, his clenched fists tucked under his armpits. He resembled the letter X. 'Babuji, my two months' salary remains unpaid. When you clear the hotel bills, please deduct ten rupees from it,' he pleaded. I assured him of my cooperation. Pleased at the prospect of earning ten rupees, he cast friendly looks at me, a smile playing on his lips. I noticed that he looked merrier than young girls, grinning literally from ear to ear.

Over the next couple of days, I managed to rent a house. As promised, before signing the bearer cheque, I brought up the issue of Sangamlal's outstanding salary. 'I'm off to Ganga Pustakalay to arrange your cheque, but it will be ten rupees short.* Isn't it true that you haven't paid Sangamlal two months' wages? He has asked me to deduct the sum from the total bill.'

The manager, who was also the owner of the hotel, summoned Sangamlal and asked point-blank, 'So, you take me to be dishonest?'

Thus confronted, Sangam froze in fear, totally tongue-tied. The owner stared hard at him for a while and then turned to me saying, 'You should pay me the money, not him. Besides, it's not wise to spoil the servants.' I handed the manager a cheque for seventy rupees and left for the newly rented house. My friend Kunwar Sahab moved with me.

One day, learning of Pagli's woes, Kunwar's maternal uncle came with a fine new blanket to be given to her. 'A quilt would have been more useful; it's cheaper than a blanket and is better at keeping out the chill,' I told Kunwar. Kunwar heeded my advice. Before setting off home for the Christmas vacation, he left his quilt for Pagli. And I lost no time in taking it to her.

---

* During his long stay in Lucknow, Nirala worked for Ganga Pustakalay (Aminabad Park), editing books and writing commentaries for *Sudha.*

Two–three days later, I ran into Shri Naitharni, my friend from the hotel. 'Pagli has been hospitalized. Doctors say she's afflicted with a double attack of pneumonia, and that she won't survive. Her child has already been sent to Shri Dayananda Orphanage. While it was being taken away, Pagli kicked up a ruckus—she wouldn't let go of her boy. A volunteer, who was the first to come to Pagli's rescue, unfazed by how untidy she was, suffered a grievous injury to his legs in the ensuing melee. He was hit by a car that drove past the tonga Pagli was being carried away on,' Naitharni reported. Some days later, Sangamlal came to me, his fists still tucked under his armpits. 'Babu, the manager encashed your cheque and ran off without paying my wages,' he complained.

'No, Sangam,' I reasoned, 'Manager Sahib is an upright man. He must have gone home to fetch more money. He needs several hundreds to settle the operational bills—for fuel, ghee, flour, milk and also for the property rent. I'm certain he'll clear your dues once he returns.'

Sangamlal heard me out, flashing that same old smile on his face.

Billesur Bakriha

Preface

Billesur Bakriha is a sketch intended to evoke laughter. I am certain it will amuse readers.[*]

25 December 1941   Suryakant Tripathi 'Nirala'
Lucknow

---

[*] Nirala describes the work as a *rekha chitra*, or sketch, implying that the story focuses more on the life and bearing of its central character—Billesur—rather than the progress of its plot. Critics have argued that 'Chaturi Chamar' and 'Devi' are also examples of rekha chitra. By that rationale, *Billesur Bakriha* can also be seen as a vivid rekha chitra of rural life in the United Provinces. The length and the expanse of the work approximate it to a novella. For the ease of reading, I have taken the liberty to add section dividers and titles to its chapters.

Preface to the Second Edition

Billesur Bakriha is a specimen of progressive literature. It has garnered fulsome praise from friends, and has also been the subject of numerous articles and reviews in print. Its first edition was sold out in no time. In this book, intimate character portraitures are implicit in the depiction of the setting itself, which is the primary attribute of progressive writing. To speak of its craft, it seems as though three short stories of varying lengths have been strung together. The end of the novel, even though conclusive enough, seems somewhat open-ended. This can shock readers yet give strength to their hearts. Please suspend your verdicts until you've read it through.

15 April 1945   Suryakant Tripathi 'Nirala'
Daraganj

1

Of Myths and Men

'Billesur' is, in fact, Villeshwar—this I learnt after quite an effort. However, the popular opinion at the place, which is located in the Poorva division, leans towards the name Billesur. Reason: Billesur is also the name of a famous Shiva shrine in Poorva. Besides, from the viewpoint of etymology, too, the word has done the place proud: you won't find a name like this elsewhere. And as for the word *bakriha*—well, at the place in question, *bakri*, or goat, is pronounced as *bokri*. Hence, bakriha becomes bokriha. However, in the story, I have stuck to bakriha, the Hindustani equivalent of the word, which is my own coinage. Here, the suffix 'ha' hasn't been used in the sense of *hanan* or loss, thereby implying the 'one who slaughters'; it is used to suggest the 'one who rears'.

Billesur is of the Brahmin caste: a Sukul from the Tari region. In the manner a person named Khayyam is taken

to be the son of a *khemewala*, a tent owner, our Bakriha
mustn't be mistaken for the son of a *bakriwala*, a low-born
goatherd. When the high-born Brahmin of Tari couldn't
find a loftier *tari*, or boat, to sail across this world, he took
to rearing goats. And so his fellow villagers conferred on
him the aforementioned title—he came to be known as
Billesur Bakriha.

There is indeed a severe drought that afflicts the land of
Hindi language and literature: *rasa* has dried up completely.
But in the everyday world of Hindi speakers, rasas flow
wide and deep, like the Ganga and the Yamuna. Perhaps
the new currents in the literature of the twentieth century
have much in common with the wonted ways of Hindi
speakers. The story of Billesur's own family fully illustrates
this: Billesur and his four brothers represent the four phases
of modern literature.

* * *

Billesur's father was called Muktaprasad. How did he
come to have such a sonorous Sanskritized name? Well,
no one really knows. His father was certainly no scholar
of the scriptures. Muktaprasad fathered four sons: Manni,
Lalai, Billesur and Dulare. Each of them was named by
the father. But apart from these proper names, each was
given a pet name, too—chosen to match the distinct
qualities they showed. Once, when Manni was barely a
year old, Muktaprasad noticed him sitting upright and
blinking rapidly, his neck raised high. That day onwards,
he started calling the child Gapuwa, which was respectfully
rendered to Gappu. Lalai, the second son, was so strikingly
fair-complexioned that his eyebrows had whitened too.

His eyes, however, were brown, and his comportment, somewhat peculiar. Hence he was named Bharra, or Bhuru for a proper name.

Owing to its divine referent—Shiva—the word Billesur itself radiates enough virtues. The father started calling him Biluwa, changed to the honorific Billu. Dulare had come into this world with a creator-willed circumcision. Understandably, the father had little difficulty picking a pet name for him; the boy was baptized Katuwa, which was refined to Kattu.

Sadly, Muktaprasad did not live long enough to see his sons grow up; he was released from his worldly cares at an early age. After Muktaprasad's demise, his wife toiled tirelessly to raise her sons; she worked the pestle, slogged in the kitchen, made cow-dung cakes, grazed the cattle, made chapattis, collected mangoes and mahua from their little orchard. And then, having introduced the brothers to the ins and outs of farming, she, too, departed to unite with her maker. But in her absence, deep differences surfaced among the brothers, and such differences impede work. As a result, the four brothers teamed up, two against two. Manni and Billesur faced off against Lalai and Dulare, forming two hostile factions within the family—like Sanatanis and Arya Samajis, the two warring sects within Hinduism. The parties remained in position for a while, but soon they splintered and branched out, like Vaishnavites and Shaivites, or Vaidiks and the ever-debating Vitandvadis. And then, to each his own tambourine, to each his own song.

* * *

Since Manni was a Sukul from Tari—supposedly inferior in the hierarchy of Brahmins—no one offered him their daughter in marriage. This aggrieved the Sanatani Manni, as his world view deemed marriage vital to one's well-being, in this world and the next. While he could dutifully offer water oblation to his departed parents at the conclusion of the *pitrapaksh*, the sacred month of the ancestors, he could not arrange the sacramental fritters for his mother's soul. Indeed, without a housewife, the home degenerates into the devil's den. Desperate for a wife, Manni went about discussing his marriage—as best he could, guided by his sense of propriety—and laid his trap wherever he chanced upon an orphaned girl.

At long last, he tasted success. Needless to say, exaggerations and plain lies clinch all such nuptial negotiations; a man worth only a penny is portrayed as a millionaire. Manni's marriage was no exception to this rule. The girl had barely stopped suckling, and her mother was a widow. 'What good is selling your daughter in marriage for two or three hundred rupees when you have to raise her for the next ten years yourself, and incur the expenses, too?' the mother was counselled. 'You should move in with someone, preferably a future son-in-law, feast on ghee, live like a queen and bring her up comfortably.' The widow took the advice to heart. Manni was nearly thirty years old, but thanks to his short height, he could pass himself off as a boy of eighteen or nineteen. And his moustache wasn't too thick to betray his age either.

There is a thicket near Manni's farm. People say it is the abode of Lord Jharkhandeshwar. One evening, Manni reached the spot, carrying every item needed to perform a puja: grains of rice, lamp, incense sticks, sandalwood paste, fruits, flowers and unction water. He squatted on his haunches and began mumbling his prayers; God alone knows what all he prayed for. Once the puja was over, he returned home, ate the prasad, lay down for a while and, before dawn broke, set out for the east. He came back a week later, accompanied by the widow and her daughter, a purple turban adorning his head.

On the way home, while they were walking past the zamindar's granary, Manni gestured towards it and declared, 'All that stock is ours.' The knowledge filled the mother-in-law with such boundless joy that she struggled to hold back her excitement. As they advanced a little further, the village orchards came into sight. 'From over there, to the other end—the entire orchard belongs to us,' explained Manni, his arm outstretched. By now, the mother-in-law was left in no doubt that Manni was an extremely wealthy bloke. It was true that his house had been divided. He now lived amid ruins, having severed all ties with his brothers. But the blessings of Vagdevi, the goddess of oratory, had been lavished aplenty on Manni; his persuasive descriptions could transform even deserted ruins into a blooming garden. Before reaching home, he led them towards the zamindar's house and said, 'This is my ancestral house, but now my brothers live here. However, I'll take you to a place more peaceful. There, you'll feel truly at home. Over here, you might not get the respect you deserve. And once we settle down, we will raise a mansion out of the wreckage.'

'Indeed, son, you are quite right: it is not wise to live among strangers,' replied the mother-in-law, brimming with adoration.

Manni took them inside his dilapidated house. Later that day, he brought five litres of milk.

'Eh, who is going to drink all that milk?' asked the mother-in-law, somewhat embarrassed.

'If we set it to simmer, its quantity will reduce by much; not a lot, considering there are three of us here. Besides, we'll also drink a little sweetened milk as sherbet, won't we?' replied Manni. The mother-in-law heaved a sigh of relief.

Manni specialized in bhang-laced thandai. He sat near the threshold of the shrine room, rolled up a bhang ball and smuggled it in, to mix it with the sweetened milk. The milk, spiked generously with bhang, was also rich in crushed almonds. The mother-in-law found its taste ambrosial and downed it in one gulp. Manni served a little to his future wife, too, and savoured the rest himself.

Having washed her hands and feet, the mother-in-law sat down to rest, while Manni busied himself frying pooris. He wrapped up all the cooking before the intoxication could hit him. Poori-bhaji, sweet milk, pickle: the whole lot was served to the mother-in-law with loving care. Thoroughly convinced that Manni was the answer to all her prayers and penance, she gorged to her heart's content. Afterwards, Manni made the bed so his mother-in-law and his future wife could rest comfortably.

Having had his dinner, Manni occupied himself with chanting God's holy name. Around midnight, he got up to check if the mother-in-law was still awake. He cleared his throat forcefully, producing quite a loud sound, but she showed no sign of having heard it; he banged the door repeatedly, but she wouldn't even twitch. He was now certain that she won't open her eyes before morning. The moment was opportune. He gently lifted his would-be wife, rested her against his shoulders and set out in the middle of the night, renouncing his home, as the Buddha once had.

By morning, he had already covered seven miles, his future wife still fast asleep. Finally, he arrived at a place where many of his relations lived. He somehow convinced them to keep quiet about the whole affair. Back at his home, when the mother-in-law finally woke up, she raised a ruckus. The scandal was out in the open; the bird had fled its coop. She wept, wailed and thumped her chest in anguish, cursing Manni bitterly: 'May you die. And your bed and body soon be cast off into the Ganga.' Having put all manner of curses on Manni, the heartbroken widow left for her home.

On an auspicious day, Manni married in secret and set out with his new wife for a new place. For the next 10–12 years, he gave his mind to raising her well and to defending dharma. Once she turned twenty, with a daughter of her own, Manni departed for his heavenly abode, leaving her all alone in this world. Manni was a devout Sanatani; men like him are known to find a place in heaven.

* * *

Lalai's story is no less strange. He came to lead a settled way of life in Ratlam, having previously tried his luck in Calcutta and Bombay, albeit without much success. Here, he became friends with a certain man who, some believed, was a Gujarati Brahmin. Sometime later, the Gujarati passed away. Alas! Such was God's will! The deceased was survived by his wife, two sons and the eldest son's wife. Lalai was left with no choice but to take over the responsibilities of the entire household. Understandably, he came to have the same kind of relationship with each of them as his late friend had. Since the family had little money in its possession, Lalai thought it wiser to return to his village than to stay on in a foreign land. As a man firm in his faith and duties, he did not distinguish between fame and notoriety; notions that bothered lesser mortals did not trouble him at all. And so he returned to his village, bringing everyone along.

When the villagers came to know of Lalai's new family—a wife, two grown-up sons and a daughter-in-law—they were wonderstruck. They hadn't seen a greater miracle in their lives, nor had they ever heard of such a thing. Lalai knew full well the consequences of attracting their attention: redemption comes hard for those whom the villagers take a fancy to. Hence, Lalai had braced himself for the coming storm, with all hopes of deliverance already forfeited. As expected, the villagers soon took to boycotting Lalai: no inter-dining, no socializing. Lalai saw some good in it, since it saved him from spending his money on fellow villagers. Before long, the villagers realized their mistake. They felt fooled, for Lalai had chanced upon a windfall, and now he could not be coerced into spending any of it on them. Meanwhile, Lalai went about his daily business quite unfazed, his conscience clear. But he waited for the right moment to improve his social standing.

Around this time, the nationalist movement swept through the country, and Lalai jumped into the fray, resolved to liberate his dear motherland. His eldest son from the adopted family, who worked somewhere in Gujarat, sent money for household expenses. Gradually, Lalai rose in esteem, and the same villagers who had spurned him came under his influence; they could not resist, even with their 'non-cooperation', the magnetic pull of Lalai's prosperity. These days, they are desperately proposing truce, while Lalai has cemented his position in the community; he has earned great renown as a political reformer.

The story of Billesur's life will be recounted later. In his case, the story carries associations with both *bil*, or a burrow, and *Ishwar*, God.

Dulare was an Aryasamaji. At the age of fifty, Bastidin Sukul had married a widow. However, he died within a year of the marriage. Sensing an opportunity, Dulare approached the widow and explained that if a husband failed to provide for his wife for three years, or even three months at a stretch, the wife had every right to take another husband. And, in her case, since Bastidin was already dead, she was free to choose a third. He also convinced the widow that he was ready to serve her in every way possible. Since a woman needs a man to lean on, the widow agreed. Sadly, Dulare himself took leave of life within a year, but not before impregnating his wife. A few months later, a son was born. These days, the child squats and plays at Lalai's threshold, like the celestial minstrel Naarad, always at another's doorstep. His mother is dead too.

2

Bengal Calling

Manni had shown the way; Billesur followed him. He had heard the villagers say that money earned in Bengal lasted long while that made in Bombay didn't. So to Bengal he went. A few from the neighbouring village were in the employment of Burdwan Maharaja—as sepoys, servitors and *jamadars*, or headmen. With bated breath, Billesur resolved to go to Burdwan. Sadly, he had no money to meet the expenses of the journey. But whoever could impede the march of a *pragatisheel*, a person of progressive temperament? Even though very few had heard of Bolshevism back then—Billesur is yet to hear the word—the idea dawned upon him automatically. He reached Kanpur, dressed in rags, and from there boarded a Calcutta-bound train, travelling without a ticket. By the time the train reached Allahabad, the ticket checker kicked him out. True to the spirit prevalent in the country back then, Billesur, too, decided to defy the law in a civil manner; even though he got off the train without protesting, he didn't discard the hallowed principle of civil disobedience.

Pacing up and down the platform, he kept asking around for directions, trying to figure out the railway routes. When another east-bound train arrived, he hopped on, only to be deboarded by Mughal Sarai. Travelling in this manner, boarding and deboarding a few more times, he reached Burdwan in 2–3 days.

* * *

Pandit Sattideen Sukul was a jamadar in the service of the maharaja of Burdwan. Even though Bengalis had difficulty pronouncing 'Sattideen'—they called him 'Satyadeen' or 'Satideen' instead—they could not raise roadblocks in his relentless march towards progress. Thanks to his sheer stupidity, he got appointed as the king's treasurer. Actually, only half a treasurer; half because while he was entrusted with the treasury keys, the accounts were kept by another babu. Sattideen, however, attributed this to his personal integrity; to his mind, he was as the only trustworthy man around. His self-belief made an impression on other Hindustanis too; people saw him as upright and dependable. Dwelling at length on Sattideen's fine reputation, Billesur sought his patronage.

Sattideen lived with his wife and a few cows. His wife was a *shikharidashna*, meaning two of her incisors were abnormally large and always visible. Much as she tried to conceal them with lips pressed together, they would stick out all the same. As a Sukul from Painku, Sattideen was superior to Billesur in the hierarchy of Kannaujiya Brahmins. Naturally, in Sattideen's home, Billesur felt 'safe' in every sense of the word.

* * *

Billesur began living with Sattideen, observing the true etiquette of a poor man's life—nimble, noiseless steps to avoid drawing attention to himself, hungry tummy tucked in, spine bent and gaze lowered in obeisance. In Billesur, Sattideen's wife found someone to pamper her in the bloom of her youth. For the first few days, she didn't mind feeding him. Then, one day, Billesur was given the chance to make himself at home in the woman's quarters. Thereafter, she cornered him and said in a nasal twang, 'I say, Billesur, now that you're here, and are likely to stay on, why don't we let the cowherd go? He is anyway a freeloader. Does he look busy doing work? Besides, there is barely any work that needs to be done. There are these clumps of standing grass over there; one just has to go, cut and bring over a load or two. And then there are those rice straw bundles, neatly tied. These are not like the straw we get back in our region. Just chop them coarsely and mix them with hay and water—the cow feed is ready. Unlike in our part of the world, here, one doesn't need to run round the cattle carrying lathis while they graze. Things are much simpler— you've got long ropes, only three cows to look after and tall standing grass. Take the cows out, tether them to a peg and let them graze on their own. When evening falls, stroll back to the pasture, like a lordly babu, bring the cows back and milk them. Life can't be easier! And if the mosquitoes come swarming at night, burn a little green straw and smoke them away. You see, it took me more time listing the chores than you will take to complete them.' Saying this, Sattideen's wife looked the other way and began pressing her lips together, trying hard to hide her incisors.

Billesur was alarmed at the proposition. He hadn't come all this way, undertaking that long, perilous journey, just to graze cattle; a work of this nature could be easily found in the village itself. But then, he was in *pardes*, an alien land, with no one to call his own, in need of someone's help to sail through these uncertain tides. He thought of taking up the work until he got a real job. And if he didn't get one, he'll go back home. So he thought to himself.

It took Billesur quite a while to frame an answer. However, by the time Sattideen's wife turned around, he was ready with his reply, 'Indeed, it's not much work. After all, it's for work alone that I have travelled seven hundred *kos*. Our place is that much far, isn't it?'

Quickly undermining Billesur's confidence, Sattideen's wife said, 'Has to be more than that—the distance between Kanpur and Burdwan.' After giving it some more thought, she added, 'I'll ask the jamadar once he returns. It's all written in his diary.'

Billesur kept quiet, cursing his luck.

The jamadar came home in the evening. Dinner was ready. His wife helped him wash his feet, after which he sat on a wooden plank, ready to eat. The poor wife, who twiddled her thumbs all through the day, now sat facing the husband dutifully. 'Jamadar,' the wife said, 'Billesur says our village is seven hundred kos from here, but I say it's farther. What does your diary say?'

Sattideen had been entrusted with a diary, but it was that other babu who maintained it. Besides matters of account-keeping, a few other things were scribbled in it. Sometimes, Billesur would ask the babu to read it out and try to make sense of it, all by himself. Sattideen harboured the belief that not only had the maharaja given him a high office but he had also put the entire world in his care, as though it was nothing but a fistful of berries. Sometimes, he brought the diary home and narrated to his wife all that he had heard from the babu, or whatever he remembered thereof.

Twirling his moustache with his left hand, Sattideen swallowed the morsel in his mouth and said, 'Allahabad alone is seven hundred kos from here.' The wife turned her victorious gaze to Billesur, her eyes glinting.

'It must be right, if the book says so,' Billesur said, conceding defeat.

Finding the husband in good humour, the wife made her submission, keeping to the same tactics as used in the olden days: first study the mood of the provider, only then make a plea. As for Billesur, he simply looked on with the crazed eyes of a needy man. Taking note of an area of improvement in his wife's sensible proposal, Sattideen modified it slightly and said, 'There is no doubt that Billesur is our man, but it is equally doubtless that he'll eat more than that boy. So, I won't pay him a wage. But he can have both his meals with us. In place of a wage, I'll tell the tehsil jamadar to let him deliver the official letters to the agents, which he'll manage in four–five hours. This way, he'll earn four–five rupees every month and keep working for us as well.'

When the modified proposal was announced, Sattideen's wife looked at Billesur with the condescending gaze of a benefactress. Billesur burst with joy at the promised meals and the monthly income of 4–5 rupees, but he concealed his feelings thinking much was still left to be accomplished. With these thoughts playing on his mind, he turned to Sattideen's wife, expressing gratitude with his eyes. Having finished his dinner, the jamadar got up to wash his hands.

3

Cows, Letters and Humble Expectations

Billesur launched himself in the battlefield called life. Many things about the cow business that were unknown to him now surfaced. Collecting cow dung, cleaning the cowshed, sprinkling ashes on cow urine, shaping cow dung cakes and giving the cattle the occasional wash—the trade had many hidden tasks.

But all this labour notwithstanding, there was no getting away from delivering letters. As instructed by Sattideen, he had to make deliveries in the nearby areas. For every delivery, he earned three annas. It wasn't long before Billesur discovered that deliveries to distant places fetched twice the money. And so he demanded those posts too. But the tehsil jamadar wouldn't have it. 'You're neither an employee nor a substitute. Moreover, Sattideen has explicitly forbidden this. I won't give you letters for distant destinations,' he argued.

Billesur fell to his knees in supplication and pleaded, 'You alone have the authority to employ me here. Until I'm officially your servant, please let me carry those other letters too. I promise to complete the twelve-kos round trip in six hours.' The headman gave in and heeded his plea.

* * *

Billesur's engagement with this letter-delivery business irked Sattideen's wife. Whenever he returned after making the deliveries, he was greeted by her arched brows, even though he never neglected his daily chores. By ten in the morning, he would wrap up everything. Once back, he would untie the cows, set them to graze and wait on them till nine in the night. Yet, Sattideen's wife never stopped complaining. Since Billesur's services came cheap, she wouldn't replace him with another servant either. Sometimes, she said hurtful things that caused his stomach to churn in revolt, but Billesur tolerated all her atrocities.

During the summer, he would attend to housework till ten or twelve. Thereafter, he would arrange the letters and set off scampering in the harsh sun, without a turban or an umbrella to cover his head, afraid he was late for work. And as soon as he got back home—panting, dry-mouthed, lips parched, body soaked in sweat and his heart pounding— he would get on with the remaining chores. Whenever he slumped to the floor, seeking a moment of respite, Sattideen's wife would lash out at him with her sharp-tongued query: 'Billesur, how much money did you make today?' On such occasions, Billesur would rein in his anger and respond with a fake sheepish grin, somehow acting coolly in that simmering heat. After resting for a while, he would once again return to the cow business and run about the house, fulfilling his numerous duties.

Those days, Billesur went around telling people that it was better to be a woman than a man, even though none understood that poignant truth. Suffering in silence, he could only summon a defeatist smile on his shrivelled lips. Back in his village, too, Billesur was in the habit of suffering quietly; he never grumbled about anything, stoically flipping through the book of his life, his world view more agnostic than a scientist's.

Holding the world in perpetual suspicion, he had come to acquire an odd visage. But even so, he chose not to give up on life, displaying the fortitude of a lonely swimmer battling the harsh currents. He didn't let Sattideen's wife get any whiff of his 'long-distance affairs'. For her, he ran only six kos, not twelve. Having rummaged through life, Billesur had cracked the code on pleasing the world. Keeping his emotions in check, he persevered for several months. Then, one day, finding the tehsil officer in an agreeable temper, he pleaded, 'Baba, please take me in your employment.'

'Fair enough! Come tomorrow for the height test,' the officers consented.

But Billesur was, after all, Manni's brother, just over five feet tall. Feeling certain that he would fail the height test, he devised a plan. He padded up the inner soles of his leather shoes—fitted already with one-and-a-half-inch heel—with layers of cotton. When he stepped into his modified shoes, he felt as if he had mounted a pile of bricks. But the feeling didn't embarrass or scare him. He reported for the test resolutely, as though he was answering a sacred call of duty. A measuring rod was brought from the law court and pressed against his frame. Billesur looked up to check if he was up to scratch. Sadly, the man tasked with measuring declared him to have fallen short by an inch and a half.

Billesur turned to the officer, pleading silently with his panic-stricken eyes. The officer smiled at him and said reassuringly, 'Billesur, there's always a position that needs deputizing; some sepoy or another is always on leave. Moreover, the wages of those on leave without pay shall be yours for the asking.'

To Billesur, the prospects augured a promotion at the workplace. He flashed a smile of contentment. And thus a year went by.

4

What Jagannath Said

Although Sattideen's wife had been married for many years, she was yet to visit Puri to have an auspicious darshan of Lord Jagannath. There was no dearth of resources either. One day, she complained to her husband, 'We have so much wealth, but no children. Once we are gone, our money will be of no use. I've been here for so long now, yet not once did I get to visit Lord Jagannath's shrine. This year, I want to seek his darshan and supplicate, "O Lord, bless me with a child and I shall grovel at your feet with an offering of sweet sheerni worth hundred and one rupees." Come to think of it, whatever could a man offer to propitiate Him? He is, after all, the Lord of the universe. Yet, I have a feeling Jagannath will grant my wish. People from all over the country flock to him and get their wishes granted.'

And then, suddenly, God alone knows with what all thoughts playing on her mind, she broke into tears.

Wiping her eyes dry with her hands, she voiced her grievances, her speech punctuated by loud hiccups. 'I have all the comforts in the world. I'm blessed with a wonderful husband and an equally wonderful family. I've got everything—money, prestige, jewellery, expensive clothes. Even my bosom is swollen with maternal love. And yet...' She broke into sobs again, longing for a child.

Sattideen drew her to his chest in a warm embrace and spoke with tender affection. 'You aren't past your prime yet. Had the first wife grieved like this, it would have made sense. Poor woman! She worked herself to death. But I married you only five years ago. How old are you now? Twenty?'

'I'm running the nineteenth,' she answered between sobs, even though she was well above twenty-five.

'Then?' asked Sattideen, 'why are you so impatient? I'm not yet old either. Besides, children come when they want to be born into this world.'

'Don't say that,' the wife cut in. 'Say they're born only when Lord Jagannath wills it.'

At this Sattideen turned somber and said, 'I see his will everywhere. I've come to hold such a high office—this, too, is Lord Jagannath's will. He resides in our hearts; we get His darshan every day. As for visiting His city, we'll surely go. I'll apply for a ten-day leave. That's no big deal.'

The wife felt somewhat reassured. Just then Billesur showed up. 'Billesur, will you come with us to Jagannath Temple?' Sattideen asked.

Billesur didn't want to add to his expenses. Sattideen could grasp his conundrum at once. 'How much money could Billesur have saved anyway?' Sattideen thought to himself. 'If he comes along, all his expenses will have to be provided for.'

However, Sattideen needed a servant for the trip. 'All right, get a ten-day leave sanctioned. We'll leave next Sunday,' Sattideen said, having thought the matter through.

Ever since Billesur started deputizing for those on leave, he was required to maintain regular attendance at the court. Naturally, Sattideen had to employ another servant to look after the cattle. While Billesur continued attending to many of the outdoor duties, as he would earlier, he lived independently and maintained a separate kitchen.

Realizing that a free pilgrimage to Puri was in the offing, Billesur was ecstatic and promptly got his leave sanctioned. The following Sunday, in the company of Sattideen and his wife, he set out for Lord Jagannath's darshan. He was to be their guard, tasked with safeguarding their belongings. Just as Sattideen's wife held that she would get pregnant once Lord Jagannath blessed her, Billesur, too, believed that he would become a permanent employee once Sattideen so much as wished for it—even if he failed the height test by a palm's measure instead of an inch and a half. Throughout the journey, Billesur kept thinking of strategies that might help him realize his dream.

* * *

Puri enthralled Billesur; from Kanpur to Burdwan, he hadn't beheld a sight so spellbinding. Breezy seashore, mounds of sand—the view was mesmerizing. But the sight of the sea was the most captivating; it filled him with uncontrollable ecstasy. He hoarded lots of snails, including some small conch-shaped ones, his heart warmed contemplating Jagannath's bounty. Thereafter, he roamed about the city, visiting landmarks like Markandey, Vatvriksh, Chandantalab. In the courtyard of the main temple, there were several smaller temples too. One by one, he visited each of them. There was one with Goddess Ekadasi's image, albeit hung upside down; it made him laugh. 'It is on Jagannath's command that Ekadasi has been hung upside down; in this land, no one is allowed to observe a fast in her honour,' Sattideen pontificated. But Billesur bowed to Ekadasi all the same.

Next, they went to see the statue personifying Kalyug, the epoch of the fallen. Kalyug held his wife aloft on his shoulders, taking care she doesn't tire herself walking, while his old father hobbled beside him. Sattideen's wife was smitten by the sculpture. Having spent several joyous days in Puri, they prepared to leave for Bhubaneswar.

In the land of Lord Jagannath, the concept of *joothan* is not known; eating someone's leftover food is quite common. Those who live chained to the sanctity of the kitchen in their homes, observing unbending purity norms, show no hesitation in sharing food with others in Puri; here, no one fusses over such restrictions. Once, while eating, Billesur used his soiled hands to serve rice into the leaf plate the jamadar and his wife were eating off. But they didn't seem to mind at all and continued gorging on the food merrily.

* * *

The following happened a couple of days later. The jamadar had had his bath. Once Billesur returned after his, he went straight to the jamadar, clung to his feet and fell prostrate in supplication.

'What's the matter, Billesur? What is it?' inquired the jamadar, sounding suspicious.

'Nothing in particular, Baba. Please help me sail across the *bhavasagar*, this treacherous ocean of life,' answered Billesur, his tone dolorous.

'But, Billesur, how can someone like me rescue you from the bhavasagar? What's wrong with you?' Sattideen was visibly worried.

'Baba, bless me with your wisdom, give me your guru mantra,' Billesur pleaded, still clinging to the jamadar's feet.

'Arre, this city is teeming with gurus, each wiser than the other. Seek a guru mantra from whomever you like,' explained Sattideen, trying hard to extricate his feet from Billesur's grasp.

'To me you're the wisest of them all. Have mercy on me,' cried Billesur and placed his forehead on Sattideen's feet.

'I don't have any guru mantra to impart. The only mantra I've ever known is the Gayatri Mantra,' said Sattideen, visibly irritated.

'Baba, no mantra is mightier than the Gayatri Mantra. I'll embrace it as the supreme gift from you, my guru,' Billesur pressed forth.

'But surely you've heard it already, during your sacred-thread ceremony.'

'I don't remember any of it. It's true, I swear by your pious feet. Last night, Lord Jagannath appeared in my dream and said . . . But wait, if I narrate it, the dream won't come to fruition.'

Sattideen's wife was thrilled to hear about the dream The purpose of the pilgrimage stands fulfilled for Billesur, she thought. She called out to him and said, 'Billesur, let go of his feet. Since Jagannath has already appeared in your dream, mark my words, the jamadar can't deny you the guru mantra. For now, come with me and tell me all about your dream in private.'

Since he had been promised a guru mantra, Billesur released his grip on Sattideen's feet and followed his wife to her room.

Billesur truthfully narrated the entire dream. 'I had sunk into a deep slumber. All of a sudden, I saw a fire flare up. Therein sat a three-faced man who said, "Billesur, you are a poor Brahmin, ill-treated by the world. But don't you worry. Serve with all your heart the one you've come with and take the guru mantra from him in Puri itself. You'll prosper and flourish." And then, all of a sudden, He disappeared—there was no one.'

Sattideen's wife was convinced that there had been a mix-up; the merits of the pilgrimage had been remitted to the wrong person and that Jagannath should have visited her in a dream, not Billesur. Perhaps there was some lapse on her part. To atone for her sins, she pledged to light a ghee-fuelled lamp every Monday in the deity's honour.

She also asked Sattideen to impart the guru mantra to Billesur. Sattideen agreed without fuss. He, in turn, asked Billesur to purchase the articles needed for the ritual—a bead necklace, a rosary, sweets, *angochha*. Elated, Billesur ran down to the market and returned with everything in a flash. Thereafter, chanting the Gayatri Mantra, Sattideen initiated Billesur into the life of a disciple. This was Billesur's second initiation with the Gayatri Mantra.

* * *

Billesur's devotion-drenched eyes impressed Sattideen's wife. Finding her own Jagannath darshan to be quite dull compared to Billesur's, she expressed yet another wish to the jamadar. 'Jamadar, shouldn't I take a guru mantra too?'

'All right, when a pandaji comes this way, we'll ask him,' answered Sattideen.

By the grace of God, a pandaji showed up just then. Sattideen humbly submitted his plea. Pandaji took a good look at Sattideen's wife and said, 'At the moment, you're unfit to bear the sacred guru mantra. You're still menstruating.'

Sattideen's wife was distraught; she stared at the pandaji with angry eyes. But the pandaji had an explanation. He told Sattideen that in a woman's case, a guru mantra proves propitious only in the fourth stage of her life. Till the time she menstruates, she is not just unclean but is also likely to give in to the temptations of the world; she can't be steadfast in protecting the sanctity of the mantra. The explanation convinced Sattideen.

The trio then travelled to Bhubaneswar before returning to Burdwan.

5

Whither Guru?

For the next one year, Sattideen's wife kept putting Jagannath's divinity to the test. On Mondays, she offered a ghee-filled diya unfailingly and waited till the end of each month for some miracle to happen. But nothing she did bore fruit. Meanwhile, Billesur's own daily observances had lengthened noticeably. Inflamed by the brilliance of tilak, beads and the Gayatri Mantra, the godly aura about him glowed brighter with each passing day.

However, when Jagannath declined to bless Sattideen's wife with a son, even after a whole year of penance and devotion, she raged at the Lord. Like the realist writers of our time, she dismissed the idea of divine intervention, becoming a votary of human agency instead.

Billesur, too, was full of regrets. He hadn't prospered one bit, and people had begun to ridicule his guru-mantra. Under these circumstances, he resolved to return to his village; slaving for the guru had proven to be far more excruciating than slaving for the zamindar had been. Besides, the weather in his village was more pleasant, and one would get to live among one's own people.

Of late, he was also irked by the godless realism of his guru's wife. One day, having made up his mind, he approached her, carrying his bead necklace and prayer rosary, and surrendered them to her. 'I've taken leave from the tehsil office to go to my village. I can't say whether I would return at all. So here is the *kanthi* and the *mala*. I won't remain a disciple any more,' he said. 'For me, you and Guru are the same. Hence I'm returning this guru mantra to you.'

Saying this, he recited the Gayatri Mantra one last time and left. After that day, he did not bow to his guru ever again.

6

Between Goats and Bullocks

Billesur returned to his village. He had money tucked in the folds of his dhoti and a confident smile on his lips. The zamindar, the moneylender and his neighbours—everyone eyed him with envy. 'How much money he must've made,' they began making wild guesses. The vast expanse of their hearts echoed with an unspoken yearning: May Billesur lose all his money. All the petty village thieves—those who used lathis to steal into mud houses at night, slip into courtyards and decamp with everyday things and old clothes—sought an opportune moment to raid his house.

One day, having firmed up his resolve to dig deeper, Trilochan met him and struck up a conversation, his tone dripping with intimacy and his 'third eye' alert to possible clues. 'I say, Billesur, do you plan to stay back in the village or would you go away again?'

Billesur knew by heart the complete life story not only of Trilochan but also of his father. However, unlike the decorated Hindi poets writing blank verse, who recite the same poem wherever they are invited, he didn't take pleasure in repeating those ugly histories at public or private gatherings. 'Bhaiya,' answered Billesur calmly, 'I've decided to settle down here in the village. In any case, the water of Bengal is bad for one's health.'

The news made Trilochan's 'third eye' gleam with enthusiasm. He moved a step closer and spoke sympathetically, like a guru speaking to his favourite disciple. 'Good, that's very good. What profession will you take up?'

'I haven't thought about that yet,' answered Billesur, smiling as before.

'Without a source that replenishes it, even a deep well dries up eventually. How long would you live off your savings?'

'I'm telling you the truth. That's the plan for now.'

'Don't you ever say that again. These villagers are real rascals. They'll report you to the police, and your name will be put down in the list of petty criminals. The right thing to say is, "Once my savings are exhausted, I'll work and earn a livelihood."'

Billesur panicked picturing the possibility. 'You're right, Bhaiya. Times are unkind. One hopes to please the Almighty with a fire sacrifice but ends up with one's fingers singed. People will say: "What does he live off if he doesn't earn anything? He must be a thief."'

Trilochan could easily sense Billesur was quite shrewd and wouldn't leak a hint about his savings or plans. So he decided to speak more plainly, citing examples to throw Billesur into a panic. 'Dinanath also sneered at such warnings, just like you. His name was added to the record of criminals. He is now kept under watch at nights,' informed Trilochan.

But Billesur still managed to sidestep the trap. He said, 'Those in the police are very discerning. Who's honest and who isn't, they can tell by simply looking into a person's eyes. While I was away, I'd given my land to Ramadin on *batai*. I'll take that back from the sharecropper and start farming myself.'

At last, Trilochan found a vague clue. 'Yes, now this is a noble plan. But you don't own a bullock. How would you till your farm?'

Billesur found himself in a spot. But he gathered his wits and said, 'That's why I said I haven't decided yet.'

Trilochan was about to fly into a rage. But that wouldn't have served any purpose beyond a belligerent outpouring of bitter words and a consequent severance of all ties with Billesur. He somehow reined in his true feelings and spoke patiently, 'You can take my bullocks.'

'But how will you manage then?'

'I want to buy a stronger pair. But I will charge you a hundred rupees for the pair.'

Billesur figured that it wasn't a bad deal. 'All right, I'll get back to you tomorrow,' he promised.

* * *

Trilochan excused himself on the pretext of a chore that needed his attention. But he was sure that a man who could pay Rs 100 at one go would have at least Rs 500–700 on his person. He left to consult with others in the village and devise schemes to lay their hands on the remainder.

Once Trilochan was gone, Billesur went indoors. He stepped out after a while, all dressed up. When people asked him where he was headed, he said, 'To the patwari— the land record keeper.'

At sunset, people saw Billesur walking back to his home, accompanied by three large pregnant goats and a man. The entire village was agog with the news. Everyone sighed with envy.

When Trilochan learnt about the goats, he came to him again and said, 'I'm glad that you brought these goats. You'll soon have a sizeable herd.'

'Yes, but I have given up the idea of buying bullocks. Who'll look after them? As for the goats, I'll simply gather leaves and feed them. With bullocks tethered at your house, you need to toil like one yourself.'

'And what about farming?'

'As I had told you, land was leased on batai. I'll bring it under *sajha* and farm in partnership.'

7

Leafing through Life

To collect leaves from goolad, peepal, pakar and other tall trees, Billesur devised a *lagga*; he fastened a sickle to one of the ends of a long bamboo pole and a hook to the other. By the time he had made the necessary preparations, the sun was already up. He set out to graze his goats, taking the path that ran through the village. Soon, he bumped into Ramdeen. 'Is it proper that a Brahmin keeps goats? However, your goats look healthy. They'll yield a lot of milk. Within a couple of years, your house will be teeming with goats and billies. You'll surely make a good profit,' Ramdeen remarked, casting a covetous gaze on the goats.

Since Billesur was on his way to work, he did not bother to give an answer. He simply held his breath and moved ahead. 'If Brahmins have taken to farming and selling shoes when in crisis, what's so shameful about goat-keeping?' he thought to himself. Up ahead he saw

Lalai Kumhar, the potter, working on his wheel. Happy at seeing the goats, he encouraged Billesur in the manner of a true comrade. Buoyed by Lalai's approving words, Billesur marched on. A temple lay ahead, with Lord Shiva reigning over the sanctum sanctorum and a statue of Mahavirji presiding over the vast stretch behind the main structure. Even though Billesur had already surrendered his guru mantra, he had no hesitation stepping inside the temple precincts and praying for the safety of his goats from wolves.

To him, Mahavirji appeared more powerful than Lord Shiva. It's likely that his preference for Lord Hanuman was tactical; standing near His statue, he could keep an eye on his goats sauntering across the passage. So he touched Mahavirji's feet and, after a quiet prayer, trod on following his goats. One of his goats charged greedily at a bordering farm. Shepherding it back to the right path, he fixed his gaze straight ahead and pressed on.

* * *

He stopped near Mannu's pucca well and with his sickle-fitted lagga, hacked down a few tender branches of the peepal that canopied the street. The moment the branches hit the ground, the hungry goats pounced on the leaves. Having cut plenty of branches for the herd, Billesur stood the lagga against a strong branch of the tree, climbed the parapet of the well and sat watching his goats serenely.

Across the path lay a piece of fallow land, along which ran a nullah. Quite a few cowherd boys had gathered there, occupying different parts of the grazing area with their cattle. The boys took due notice of Billesur's arrival. They also saw his goats, whom they wanted to shoo away. To this end, the older ones among the boys got into a huddle to conspire against him. They decided to lead the goats towards the nullah. It would set Billesur worrying, and he would search around frantically for his goats, the boys imagined. If he found them, well and good; if he didn't, they couldn't care less. 'And if we clue the Pasis in,' one of them suggested, 'they'll butcher the goats in the nullah itself; some meat will come to our share too.' Another objected saying, 'They're pregnant. What use would their meat be?' Even so, the boys couldn't deprive themselves of the thrill of chasing the goats away.

Following careful deliberations, a few walked up to Billesur, while others kept an eye on the goats. One of them broke the ice and said, 'Kaka, come, let's play a game.'

Billesur smiled at the suggestion and spoke mockingly, 'Go, call your father. Are we the same age that we should play together?' And then he turned his attentive gaze towards his goats.

Another said, 'All right, Kaka, don't play with us if you don't want to. You've lived in *pardes*. Pray tell us something interesting about that foreign land.'

'No one gets to see heaven without actually dying. When you grow old and travel, you'll learn all about pardes yourselves,' Billesur explained calmly.

'Don't worry, the wolf never comes down to this place; it prowls only at that farm up there,' observed a third, trying to get Billesur to let his guard down.

'He comes here, too, but disguised as a human,' said Billesur and got up to leave.

* * *

The goats had munched off every single leaf on the branches. Billesur picked up his lagga with a flourish and guided the herd to the other side of the field. Moving in the direction of the orchard, upwards from the grazing land, he chopped off some vines from reeyan climbers.

On his way back to the village, he ran into Deenanath. 'How much did you pay for them?' asked Deenanath, eyeing the goats greedily.

Reading the greed in his eyes, Billesur replied, 'Got them for *aadhiya*—half the ownership, half the risk.'

Billesur's spell of good fortune sent a shock of envy running through Deenanath's body, all the way to his tuft. 'All three for aadhiya?' asked Deenanath in a tone full of surprise.

'Indeed. What did you think—only one?' Billesur answered, wearing his typical smile.

'You mean the goats are yours, the milk is yours, and if they die, the risk is his. Ownership of the kids, fifty-fifty?' Deenanath asked, dwelling on the details.

'Yes.'

Already green with envy, Deenanath felt doubly crushed imagining the size of Billesur's possible profits. 'Right, it is for Him to lavish boons,' he muttered jealously. 'So, Billesur will have all the fun by himself, eh? Well, if I don't gorge on his goats, call me unworthy of my name.'

Billesur noticed furrows of agitation lining Deenanath's forehead; his eyes suggested that he had resolved to wreck Billesur.

Billesur stumbled routinely along the highway of life; sometimes he kept his balance, sometimes he fell flat. Of late, he was being extra cautious, his vigilant gaze fixed on the road ahead. He made his way decisively to a goolad tree, cut some more leaves and tied them into a bundle to feed the goats later at home. When the goats had had their fill, he returned home taking a different route, with the bundle balanced atop his head.

8

Being Bakriha

Billesur's own house had been partitioned off so many times that it was impossible for him to live there with his goats. Besides, since his brothers weren't suffering from tuberculosis—meaning they had no use for the medicinal goat milk—they would have surely objected to the stench of the goats. Furthermore, on account of being old, the house had caved in at many places. At night, thieves could raid in the guise of wolves and make off with the goats. For many such reasons, Billesur decided to stay in an old unoccupied house in the village. But he did not buy it; he was allowed to move in on the condition that he would thatch it, repair it and save it from collapsing. He also promised to vacate it at six months' notice. The owner lived in pardes; in a way, he had settled there for good. And the custodian of the house, having pocketed a princely bribe of sixteen annas, had shown Billesur great kindness.

The fact that the house belonged to a pardesi didn't mean that it was more elegant or comfortable. When the pardesi lived in that house, he too, like Billesur, was a desi. It was the abject poverty of the *des*—the province of his ancestors—that had driven him away to pardes. The house stood facing a dark, deep well and a tamarind tree. Its rain-washed walls had bloated so unevenly that it seemed as if spouts had been bored through them. Since the inner drains were choked, rainwater would flow out through the door, making a pit near the threshold. Over time, the pit had grown so large that even animals as big as dogs could slip through it. The ground around the threshold was evenly uneven; one couldn't even balance a cot on it, let alone spread a mattress to sleep on the surface. At the farther end of the house, there was a small courtyard, with a smallish room attached to it. Billesur chose this room to live in. He filled the pit under the door and continued to repair the house gradually.

For over a year, he lived frugally, cooking once and splitting his meal, but his ambitions and work, both kept growing. At the same time, obstacles continued to plague him. Among all the people in that village, not one was his friend; it seemed as though he lived in a citadel full of enemies. So hostile was the place that one couldn't count on even one's own brothers. Billesur often wondered why the villagers never stood by one another, but he found no satisfactory explanation to this sad mystery. It is possible that his failure to unravel the mystery of this perennial hostility had enabled him to grasp the ways of the world.

'Even so, as long as a man breathes, he has to work, help others, seek support—this is the truth about life.

But no one seems mindful of this simple fact. This condition seems hopelessly doomed.' Billesur, our very own Socrates, did not command the eloquence to philosophize like a sophist, but his philosophy wasn't a shallow one. It's just that no one ever valued his wisdom. Since Billesur himself could never find his way out of this vicious maze, he kept rambling about.

* * *

Some more time passed. Billesur continued to live with the goats, in a house littered with goat droppings. He had always been of a strong build. With goat milk now available in abundance, he only grew stronger. By now, several grandkids were born to the goats he had initially bought. He had also managed to sell a few billy goats. His earnings looked good.

Naturally, he was an eyesore in the village. Once, some villagers approached the zamindar and complained that since Billesur's goats had shorn all the trees down to mere stumps, he should be made to sell them off. 'Okay,' said the zamindar, at first encouraging the villagers, only to put the matter off eventually. Since he had already taken note of what Billesur's goats were up to, he had started extracting a fixed sum from Billesur for trimming the government trees down. The dejected villagers took their frustration out on Billesur by bestowing on him the belittling moniker 'Bakriha'. In retaliation, Billesur began naming the goat kids after the villagers.

9

When the Night Descends

Having bathed, cooked, eaten and saved a little for the evening, Billesur stepped out with his goats, balancing the lagga on his shoulders. It was the season of ripening jamun. He hooked his lagga to a branch and gave it a nice judder. Fruits rained down. He collected them in his *angochcha* and moved ahead, relishing the juicy berries as he went about his daily business.

A little further down was the Mahavir temple. He scaled the low platform built around it, spat out a jamun stone, touched the feet of the statue and mumbled his usual prayer: 'O Lord, keep protecting my goats.' Sadly, Billesur wasn't blessed with the *antardrishti* of Tulsidas or Sitaji; if only he had such an 'inner eye', he would have seen that the statue of Mahavirji had smiled at him. Having rushed through all his prayers, he jumped down the platform and led his goats along the trail leading to the orchard.

It was already afternoon. Since it had poured down in torrents, the soil was all soaked. Ponds, pools, pits and ditches—everything seemed brimming with water. All the farmers keen on sowing crops of their choice—cotton, rice, millets, legumes, jute plants, cowpeas, cucumber, corn, black gram, etc.—were busy plowing their fields. The balmy fragrance of moist earth that floated all about lifted Billesur's spirits. As one familiar with the ways and means of agriculture, he dreamt of a novel idea for farming even as he marched on goading his goats.

Of the fields given out to sharecropping, he had taken one back to farm himself. Monsoon farming isn't too toilsome. Plough once, space out the seeds evenly at an arm's length and let the crops grow luxuriantly with rainwater. But Billesur did not own bullocks. Moreover, no one would have lent him theirs that early in the plowing season. So Billesur decided that over the next 6–7 days, he would wield a hand plough and till his plot himself.

Even though the villagers grew a variety of crops, none sowed shakarkand or sweet potatoes. A harvest of shakarkand would fetch good profits, Billesur thought. 'And then, with the onset of winter in the month of *Agahan*, I would plant peas in the same plot. When the shakarkand saplings begin to sprout, demanding nightly vigil, I would hire someone to keep an eye on the crop.'

With these plans taking shape in his mind, he hoped to earn a handsome amount.

* * *

Billesur marched on with his goats. When he returned to his senses, having chalked out the entire course of action in his head, he suddenly realized that he had strayed far from the village. Annoyed at his own absent-mindedness, he threw a hurried gaze of inspection at the goats. Ganga, Yamuna, Sarju, Parvati—present. Sekhaen, Jameela, Gulabiya and Sitabiya were there. Ramua, Shyamua, Bhgwatiya, Parbhuwa were with the herd. Turui, too, was present. But where was Dinwa? Alarmed, Billesur looked all around, staring warily as far back as possible. But Dinwa was nowhere to be seen. His heart skipped several beats.

Deenanath, or Dinwa, was the strongest of the herd, and yet, of all the goats, he was the one who seemed to have lagged behind. Where did he disappear? He began calling after him. 'Urrrrr, urrrr . . . rr! Dinwa, come . . . take this . . . come urrrr! Come on . . . come on, Dinwa! Urrrr, urrrrr . . . Deenanath, son . . . urrrrrr!' Turui began bleating anxiously. But Deenanath did not return. 'Turui, where is Dinwa?' muttered Billesur, feeling sad and desperate. Bleating, Turui ambled close to him.

Billesur decided to gather his goats and retrace his steps. A group of boys stood by the side of the nullah, grazing their cattle. On seeing Billesur, they gave a crooked smile. Billesur was nursing a grieving heart. Their derisive grin made him seethe with fury. But he somehow kept his cool and inquired gently, like a good-natured man, 'Bachha, did one of my goats get left behind around here?'

'Which goat?'

'A strong billy goat. I called him Dinwa.'

'If you called him Dinwa, then go ask Dinwa. How would we know where he is?'

Billesur didn't probe any harder, but doubts nagged him. He thought of carrying out a thorough search near the nullah, but whom could he trust to watch over his herd? What if the boys steal another goat kid? He dashed towards his house, running his herd along. On the way, he came across a couple of curious people. 'What's the rush, Billesur? Why are you running the goats down like that?' asked a villager, appearing to be concerned.

'Bhaiya, someone has stolen one of my billy goats, over there, near the nullah. There are some boys around the place, but they wouldn't tell me a thing.'

'There are such lowly thieves in the village that even if you leave a humble pan in the courtyard, they'll climb down the terrace and run away with it. But if you confront them, they hound you around, hurling insults at you wherever you go. It's such a pity! What should the aggrieved do? Should he leave? Where shall he run away to?' explained a wise villager, painting a bleak picture of life in the village.

* * *

Billesur rushed to his house. He opened the door, locked the herd—kids in a room, goats in the open area near the door—and then set out looking for Dinwa, with a lathi in his hand.

First, he stopped at Deenanath's house. But when he learnt that Deenanath wasn't home, he took the dusty path and went straight to the nullah. A boy was sitting casually on a mound, throwing roving glances around the place. Billesur got the drift. He started scanning the entire stretch along the nullah. On seeing him approach, the boy gave a unique warning call. Billesur heard it, too. Now he had no doubt that his goat was somewhere nearby. He scurried on until he espied a bush in the distance. He had a feeling his goat must be lying dead thereabouts. However, when he reached the bush, he found nothing. Anxious, he cut through the thicket and began inspecting the spot thoroughly. The ground was soaked in blood. As the realization dawned on him, his face fell. He could feel his heart sob inconsolably, but his eyes were dry. 'There is no justice in the world; people preach but empty sermons,' he thought to himself, grieving bitterly.

He walked back to the well, feeling hot, and rested on its parapet. His billy goat had been slaughtered, and the boys knew the entire truth, but they wouldn't breathe a word about it. The animal was worth eight rupees. The thought of what he had lost broke his heart. There was no one who could help him in the matter. The setting sun beat down straight on his head, but so lost was he in his thoughts that he didn't feel its scorching rays.

Today, the goats were left hungry; it was already evening and he hadn't had the time to graze them. Since he wasn't carrying the lagga either, he couldn't collect leaves on his way back. The herd looked set to starve in the night too. How could the poor animals carry on like this? If they didn't eat at night, they would produce no milk in the morning. If that happened, the kids would go hungry and begin to lose weight. They could even take ill for want of nourishment. There was some bran at home, but that wasn't enough for the entire herd. 'So what if it's dark? I must step out and bring some twigs,' he told himself.

The sun had set, and the sadness of the dark evening descended into Billesur's eyes. The wind soughed all around. The nullah flowed on, as if spreading deathly tidings. Having ploughed their fields, farmers were trudging back to their houses, perhaps prepared to be buried and crushed under the domestic grind awaiting them. Perched on the branches their nests were built on, birds tweeted their lament: 'When the night descends, who would save us from the wild cat?' The wind carried a sad message: one day, everything would blow away, like this.

As Billesur lumbered back to the village, a lathi in hand, somehow consolation came to him by itself. His heart summoned the courage for the next task, his confidence increased automatically. When he reached the edge of the forest, Mahavirji's temple came into sight. It was already quite dark. He climbed the platform from the frontage and, having circled the temple anticlockwise—violating the sacred rule of *pradakshina*—reached the statue in the sanctum. Standing irreverently in front of Mahavirji, he spoke in rage, 'Look at me, I'm a poor man. Since people call you the protector of the poor, I used to come to you and plead, "Lord, please protect my goats and their kids." But did you, standing here with that snout, protect them? Answer me!' He got no reply. Looking Mahavirji in the eye, Billesur swung hard at the statue's face with his lathi—so hard that the idol's clay head flew off its body and landed furlongs away.

10

Ghee and Shakarkand

Billesur—as has been narrated thus far—had stared sorrow in the face many a time, challenging its menacing countenance over and over again. Not once did he concede defeat.

These days, thanks to the fact that Mahatma Gandhi drinks goat milk, there is a great demand for it in the cities; it has, in fact, become pricier than cow milk. It's possible that the fad has become popular in the villages too.

But in the times Billesur lived in, the entire world loathed goat milk. It was given only to those who were severely ill or were prohibited from drinking cow milk because of poor digestion. Unfortunately, there was none who belonged to either category in Billesur's village. Much as he tried, he could not sell the milk of his goats. There were some to whom it was given gratis, so they may socialize with Billesur. But now, even they had started twisting their faces into a wry grimace. At last, Billesur decided to condense goat milk as khoya. However, the plan faced several hurdles, which included the nature of the milk itself. Owing to its high water content, he had to use large quantities of firewood and sit stoically by the sweltering hearth for hours. The result disheartened him; for all his efforts, the yield was but a disappointingly small ball of khoya. While buffalo milk yielded a quarter per *ser*, goat milk didn't produce even half of that.

Mustering up great pluck, he went to Bhajna Halwai Jotpurwale to sell the produce. Since Bhajna was busy kneading a dough, he didn't have the time to examine the quality of the khoya. He weighed it hurriedly and paid some money to Billesur. The following day, when Billesur visited him again, Bhajna simply weighed the khoya and put it aside.

'What about the payment?' demanded Billesur.

'I made the payment yesterday itself. I thought the khoya was made of buffalo milk. Turns out it's goat milk. For khoya of this quality, even half of what I've paid you is more than fair. I don't buy such pathetic stuff; don't bring it to me ever again. It spoils all my sweets, and the customers start abusing me. It has neither fat nor taste. And the little ghee it yields can't be mixed with regular ghee; the entire lot begins to stink.'

Billesur made no fuss and returned empty-handed, his head bowed in shame. He had the goods to trade, but there were no takers. And so he came up with yet another plan, one that needed much less effort than preparing khoya. Billesur would start a fire with dung cakes and set the milk to boil. In the meantime, he would attend to other chores too. Once the milk had cooled down, it was set to curdle and, the next day, churned for butter. Billesur remembered to share the buttermilk with the goat kids. He would then extract ghee from the butter, mix it with a fourth of buffalo-milk ghee bought from the market and sell it at reduced rates. In the dehat, one can easily trade the mixed variety of ghee, prepared by mixing cow, buffalo and goat ghee. Those households with more than one species of milch animal do not curdle their milk separately.

* * *

Billesur's scheme proved a success. Rationalizing the billy goat's death as but a brief moment in the vast cosmic cycle of loss–profit–life–death, he steadily looked ahead to the future. He resolved that he wouldn't take the goats out to graze until the farm was ready and the shakarkand saplings were planted; he would feed them at home instead. Early next morning, he picked up his plough and set himself to work in the fields. The kids and goats were locked in the room and the doorway area respectively, as always. The previous evening, he had cut enough leaves and twigs to last the herd the whole day.

When the villagers saw him working a hand plough, they ridiculed him. But Billesur didn't retort to the jibes; he kept his peace and kept toiling determinedly. Before noon he had ploughed a good expanse of the land. It warmed his heart. He was convinced that with 6–7 days of labour, he would make up for the loss of Dinwa. He returned to his place in the afternoon, prepared a watery sweet porridge and gave himself a little rest after eating a mouthful.

When he got up, noon had passed but dusk was yet to set in. He got back to the fields and turned up the soil till evening, returning at the onset of night with a bundle of leaves for his goats. Working frantically, Billesur managed to plough the entire field in the space of only five days, far ahead of the seven-day target he had set for himself. He had also dug up a long furrow. When people asked, 'What do you plan to sow, Billesur?' he answered, 'Bhang.'

In dehat, everyone is wary of letting you in on their plans. Come to think of it, isn't it the same everywhere? Billesur searched around and finally found the slips of shakarkand. One day, people saw him planting the saplings. Once it rained and the saplings began to spread around, Billesur raised mounds around the area, as one does on a potato farm.

11

A Suitable Bride

Since the day Billesur had bought the goats, instead of buying bullocks from Trilochan, the latter had been looking for ways to dupe Billesur. As the goat kids grew taller, so did Billesur's standing among the rich of the village. The place was rife with all manner of opinions about him.

By the onset of the autumnal month of Kwar, Billesur's shakarkand plants were in full bloom. People began to speculate how many tonnes the yield would be. One day, while Billesur was relaxing in his room, enjoying a dough of milk-kneaded, jaggery-sweetened sattu, Trilochan showed up. A skep, used to cover the goat kids with, lay upturned nearby. Trilochan wanted to use it as a stool and sit on it, but when he noticed Billesur motion 'don't' with his hand, he happily sat on the floor instead.

'I have great news for you, Billesur,' announced Trilochan smilingly.

Billesur did not utter a word. Like a guru, he raised his palm and suggested with a gesture that Trilochan should be patient.

'So you don't talk while eating?' asked Trilochan.

Billesur nodded in the negative, his eyes shut, his visage solemn. But that did not stop Trilochan from rehearsing the conversation in his head.

Before long, Billesur finished his sattu and got up, but he was in no hurry. Sitting near the drain, he washed his hands, rinsed his mouth and, as a matter of habit, picked his teeth with the copper toothpick tied to his *janeu*, the sacred thread. He rinsed his mouth once more and, after letting out a loud burp, ambled back to the room with his head bent down. Trilochan watched him patiently. Then Billesur dragged out a cot and invited Trilochan. 'Come, sit yourself down. But be careful, don't give it a jerk.' Trilochan got up from the floor and sat on the cot. Billesur took position on its other end.

Trilochan took a good look at Billesur and then spoke, his eyes widening in excitement. 'I bring an excellent marriage proposal, if you care to consider it.'

The mere mention of marriage sent an electric current down Billesur's nerves. But as is deemed desirable in Hinduism, he viewed the whole matter in the light of the doctrine of utilitarianism and said, 'You can see for yourself. I've to make do with mere sattu. If I had a wife, she would have fed me chapattis even from her death bed.'

'That's so true,' said Trilochan, putting on a serious countenance.

Emboldened by his approving words, Billesur continued. 'I'm languishing here for the sake of the love I have for my brothers in the village. Otherwise, I can choose to live my days anywhere in the world.'

'You're telling me!'

Billesur suddenly felt his manhood stirring. 'You see, I was in Bengal. If I had so desired, I would have kept a woman. But one cannot allow the honour of one's family to bite the dust—isn't it? Why ruin it for such trifle, I thought. Had that happened, you people would have denounced me saying, "Billesur, you've sullied your father's good name."' Having sketched out the context elaborately, Billesur was hesitant to cut to the chase. He would inch closer to the subject of marriage, but edge away each time.

'The entire village praises you—not just ours, but the neighbouring ones too. They say, Billesur is a real man,' said Trilochan.

'People stake their very existence for the sake of their reputation. Why do you think I work so hard? If you don't have a fair name, you've got nothing of value. My father lives on long after he's dead. But what will happen to his name if he never has a grandson?' Billesur solemnly observed.

'There's no way a man with a son as wise as you won't have a grandson,' added Trilochan, suddenly sounding grave.

'Parents are the true gods in the world. But for them, dharma would have long disappeared from the face of the earth.'

'Indeed! Each one of us must protect our dharma. That's why the scriptures tell us to defend our faith, even if it costs us our lives,' Trilochan provided the gloss.

'Now look at my life—I go work in the fields, I come back to rest, but there's no woman around to comfort me. Without a woman tending the hearth, your food is never cooked according to the prescribed scriptural rules. Always in a tearing hurry, one never gets to bathe properly, or cook properly, or even eat the right way. What's left of dharma?' said Billesur in a tone filled with agitation.

'I learnt my lessons long back; it is now your turn to be versed in it,' said Trilochan, setting his incisive 'third eye' to penetrate and mould Billesur's mind.

Billesur cast a probing glance at Trilochan and thought to himself, 'Look at him—he came to me as a grovelling middleman but now imagines himself to be the shrewdest in the world. Soon he will demand money. God knows who she is or who her father is. There must be some flaws in her character. But the trouble is, I'm finding it difficult to get by all alone. When we feel hunger, we eat. Likewise, because it rains, the sun scorches us, and the wind blows hot, we seek shelter in a house. But to run that house properly, one needs to marry. It's true—only a wife can handle housework. After marriage, people cram their houses with all sorts of goods and luxuries, pamper their wives with jewellery. But come to think of it—isn't it all but a sham? Hollow on the inside, like a drum.'

As Billesur framed that searching question, he was reminded of his guru's wife in Burdwan. The stories he had known—of every house in the village—flashed before his eyes too. All those accounts were a far cry from the 'truth' people tell about marriages. As a snare catches innocent bulbuls, a web of lies entraps unsuspecting men. Perhaps some of Trilochan's cunning had rubbed off on Billesur. Nonetheless, as there was nothing to lose, and also because he was eager to know whatever Trilochan was up to, he spoke affectionately. 'Yes, brother, everyone in the village looks upon you as a wise person.'

Flattered by praise, Trilochan said, 'A bride like her has never graced this village—all of sixteen years, hot like fire.'

If not for the pious thoughts of virtuous goddesses that came swarming into his head just then, he would have gone berserk with joy. But he disciplined his mind and said, 'Indeed. Could your eyes ever be deceived? Which village is she from?'

'For now, I won't tell you all that. When you set out to marry her, you'll discover everything yourself.'

'Will there be *phaldaan* or would the customary lavishing of fruits and gifts be dispensed with too?'

'There will definitely be phaldaan, but no more probing around. At the moment, all I can say is that the girl comes from an upright Tiwari clan. I'll be the mediator and deal with every little detail.'

'Which village does she come from?' Billesur repeated his query.

'If I told you that, there'll be nothing left to say. Anyway, you'll surely get to know that before marriage. But there's one issue: they can't afford the wedding expenses. However, they are people of honour, they won't sell their daughter. So you'll have to meet the expenses of the ceremony.'

'How much would I have to pay?'

Trilochan did a quick calculation and elaborated, 'When they come to our village for the phaldaan ceremony, they'll put up at my place. In the offering plate, they'll present you with seven rupees in cash, a coconut and a roll of clothes. All this will cost you twenty rupees. You'll have to pay this sum seven days ahead of the ceremony. And then, once the phaldaan is concluded, you'll have to pay one hundred and fifty rupees to cover the wedding expenses. Of course, all the money will pass through my hands. They're very good people, but they don't have the resources. It will be quite embarrassing for them to speak directly to you about money matters. Considering the fact that one hundred fifty rupees cover all the ceremonial expenses—ritual welcome, marriage, feast, gifts for the groom and the baraat's send-off—what you have to pay is but a pittance. I must tell you that they don't want you to be wrecked by the expenses. But you'll do well to remember that in the clan hierarchy, they're your superiors.'

Billesur was alarmed. 'If they come from a superior clan, this marriage won't last. Look at what happened with Mannu Bajpayee—poverty forced him to get off his high horse and marry his daughter into a lower clan. His daughter is now a widow. Brother, I'm really afraid—what if . . .'

Trilochan's face fell. 'You worry for nothing. All these higher-ups are mere pretenders. In reality, they aren't so superior after all. As for Mannu Bajpayee's daughter—she killed her own husband. Rumour has it that she was already quite old at the time of her wedding and had also lost her virtue at her natal place. That was why Mannu had to compromise. People say she poisoned her husband at her lover's bidding. In any case, the husband wasn't keeping well and was on medication.'

'What if she does the same to me?' Billesur sounded concerned.

'I repeat—there's no cause for worry when I'm the go-between. The girl has no blemishes, no flaws, and her morals aren't loose. She isn't dark, blind, lame or limp.'

'I trust this since it's coming from you. But if I don't get the address, what am I to tell the relatives who'll come much ahead of the wedding. They can't be told, "Trilochan Bhaiya knows it." That's why I insist on knowing. And yes, we must also have her horoscope carefully examined. Get the girl's horoscope. I'll have it read in my own presence. What if she is a *mangali*? The hostile Mars in her horoscope will cost me my life. If one must marry, one must take every precaution too.'

In his heart of hearts, Trilochan was livid. 'You speak as if you're a prince. They didn't come to you with the proposal, nor would any other decent man. Seeing you live a vagabond's life, like a man afflicted with the cursed Bhadra *nakshatra*, I thought of helping you settle down. But you've now revealed your true colours. What if your Mars is hostile? Which father would then give his daughter to you? As for the relatives attending your wedding, I consider it foolhardy to add a pointless expense of twenty-five rupees. I suggest you get married on the quiet. If you're so keen to find out who the girl's father is, then come on, let's go to their place and meet the family. However, it won't be a decorous thing to do; the whole village will ridicule us both.'

Billesur now felt somewhat assured. Even though he was put off by the demands for money, he found himself ensnared by the description of the girl's beauty. Although a hundred flowers of marriage bloomed in his heart, their fragrance permeating all around, they didn't inspire any confidence in him; he couldn't bring himself to trust Trilochan completely. He asked, 'How far is their village?'

'About three to four kos.'

Billesur thought of making a day trip to the girl's village and returning before sundown. That way, the goats wouldn't be put through much hassle. He would stock up enough leaves for them to feed on. He said, 'All right, brother, let's go. One should see everything for oneself. Whichever day you suggest will suit me just fine.'

'Excellent! Fourth day from today,' said Trilochan, trying to read Billesur's mind.

12

A Great Deception

Billesur didn't sleep a wink that night. He kept picturing the girl's beauty. Imagining her to be very fair, he called Ramratan's wife to mind. As he meditated upon her tender age—all of sixteen—the face of Ramcharan Sukul's daughter flashed before his eyes. He pictured her eyes to be big, like those of Hasina, the daughter of Pukhraj Bai. A girl like her was sure to light up his entire house.

He thought of putting her belongings in the room where the goat kids were housed and of shifting the kids to the vacant space near the doorway. He also thought of thatching the open area, to make it comfortable for the herd all through the year. Yet, as he drew up these elaborate plans, not once did he imagine that with the stench of goat shit wafting about the entire house, a stately woman like that may not choose to spend a single day there.

The next morning, he got up early and went straight to a clothier in a neighbouring village. He bought a pink turban, a dhoti and a cloth piece for making a kurta. Giving his measurements, he instructed the tailor to stitch up the kurta the same day. He also bought a pair of shoes from the cobbler.

* * *

Even as he went about planning his marriage, he kept an eye out for Trilochan's activities. On the third day, he saw Trilochan leave his house. Looking at his dress and the lathi in his hand, Billesur could surmise that Trilochan was going to hold talks with the girl's family and that he would take him along the next day, once everything was settled. Dressed in his ordinary daywear, Billesur followed him too, keeping a safe distance to avoid being seen. Upon reaching a village called Babu Ka Purva, Trilochan left the *kachcha* road and turned towards the settlement. Taking his position on the outskirts of Purva, Billesur waited patiently for Trilochan to emerge out of the settlement and move towards another village. But when it didn't happen, Billesur was convinced that the girl lived there. Enthused, he too walked into the village.

When he ran into a villager near the exit, he was quick to inquire: 'Was a certain Trilochan from Shyampur here?'

'Yes, that thug is over there, at Ramnarayan's house. They're birds of a feather! Must be conspiring to ruin someone's life,' the man answered wryly.

Billesur's heart sank. 'Does Ramnarayan have children? Boy or girl?' he asked.

The stranger cast a look of surprise at Billesur. 'Where are you from? Don't you know Ramnarayan? The children are his brother-in-law's, from the wife's side. Well, go ahead, ask me whether or not he's married?' jeered the man and left.

Billesur felt queasy. But he kept moving in the same direction until he reached the residence of Manni's in-laws. The old mother-in-law was home. The two chatted leisurely—about happiness and sorrow, things good and ugly. Billesur consoled the woman and told her to come to him if she ever needed money. Saying this, he slipped a one-rupee note in her palm. He also shared news about Manni—that Manni was doing well and taking good care of her daughter, and that her daughter was all grown up now.

The news made Manni's mother-in-law extremely happy. She kept the money and asked if Billesur had married. 'Only parents can see to it that their children are settled,' answered Billesur gravely. Moved by his plight, the mother-in-law promised to visit him in 10–15 days and finalize his marriage. Billesur sought her blessings by touching her feet and took leave of her.

13

Tread with Caution

The following day, Trilochan came over and said, 'Billesur, get ready.'

'I'm all set already,' answered Billesur.

Trilochan was pleased to find his plan reaching fruition. 'Very well. Let us go.'

'Bhaiya, there's this girl in the family of Manni's mother-in-law's sister. They were here yesterday with a proposal. It's all settled now. Please pardon me.'

'Well, in that case, this marriage is bound to be a disgrace. And so shall be the girl. I can bet on it.' Trilochan made a dark prophecy in anger.

Billesur summoned a smile on his lips and retorted, 'And the match you've arranged is so saintly! If the girl from Manni's mother-in-law's sister's family has every shortcoming in the world, what about your girl? No one knows anything about her parentage, her village or even her own relations. Does she come festooned with a velvet tassel?'

'Look here, you're in for a terrible regret,' predicted Trilochan.

'I leave no scope for regrets. Treading with caution is a habit with me, Trilochan Bhaiya,' Billesur answered firmly.

'Okay, but at least meet the girl once. Come with me, I'll even show you the girl,' Trilochan implored in desperation.

'Even if you promise an introduction with her mother, let alone the girl, I won't come with you. If there's a worthy girl among one's own relations, one mustn't look beyond it. For it amounts to deserting one's dharma. A girl from a decent family is valued for her virtues, not for her looks. Besides, as the adage goes, a beautiful girl bears an ugly character.'

'So you're bringing home a chaste *savitri*, eh? Very well! You'll know soon enough if the village loafers leave her alone,' warned Trilochan, switching from the pronoun of endearment to the one considered offensive in Hindi.

'I'm quite aware of all this. But at least she won't run off with my possessions—mark my words. Whatever calamity befalls me, she'll weather it along. No one can corrupt someone faithful. Also, I know all about the virtues of my fellow villagers.'

'So you now accuse us of having loose morals?'

'I'm not accusing anyone. I'm merely telling the plain truth.'

'Fair enough, but you must state plainly what you're blaming me for, otherwise . . .'

'You'd better leave right away or I'll go to the police.'

Once the police was mentioned, Trilochan thought it wise to leave, but he kept scowling back at Billesur even as he walked away.

14

With Amma's Blessings

Manni's mother-in-law arrived at the beginning of Kartik. Even though she lost her way in the village, she eventually managed to find Billesur's house. The moment Billesur saw her, he threw himself at her feet. Ushering her indoors, he laid out a cot, cushioned it with a jute carpet and said affectionately, 'Amma, please sit here.'

'And you? Will you keep standing like that?' said Manni's mother-in-law, sitting herself down on the cot.

'Sons ought to stand dutifully and serve their parents. So what if you have only a daughter? It is the same with sons and daughters. Besides, as my elder brother's wife, your daughter commands my respect. You see, some consider conceiving sinful, and denounce the woman who gives birth as a sinner. But being a mother-in-law, your motherhood is sanctioned by law, by dharma itself. Please stay put, I'll come back in a moment.'

Billesur ran to the village Baniya and bought a quarter kilo sugar. Coming back, he mixed it with goat milk and kept a full *lota* by the cot's headrest. Offering a glass of water to the old lady, he said, 'Here, take this. Rinse your mouth. If you like to wash your hands and feet, there is more water in the bucket. Sit here, draw as many glassfuls as you like and freshen up.' He then picked up the milk lota and stood waiting on the old woman. Once Manni's mother-in-law had washed her hands, Billesur started pouring milk in her glass, and the old woman began guzzling it down, one glass after another. Having drunk to her heart's content, she tried to justify her self-indulgence and said, 'Bachcha, goat milk is the only milk I drink. It's extremely good for human health as it cures all the diseases from their very roots.'

Evening had descended, the sky was clear, and the tamarind tree teemed with bustling birds. Billesur looked at the sky and said, 'Amma, there's still time. You sit here and keep an eye on the goats. I'll be back in a jiffy. Or else, shut the door from inside. I'll knock when I return. Amma, one must exercise caution; this village is teeming with goat thieves.' As Billesur stepped out, Manni's mother-in-law bolted the doors.

* * *

Walking across the fields, he made straight to Ramghulam's vegetable farm. Ramghulam, a Kachchi or vegetable grower by caste, was present there.

'Which vegetables are you selling today?' asked Billesur.

'There's brinjal, there's bitter gourd. What do you want?'

'Give me a ser of brinjals and take care to get the tender ones.'

Ramghlam began plucking brinjals while Billesur looked on, marvelling at the lovely verdure of the plants growing around him. It seemed as if each plant proclaimed proudly, 'I've no peers in the world.' Having plucked and weighed the brinjals—drawing Billesur's attention to the sag in the goods side of the measuring scale—he placed the produce in Billesur's *angochcha*. Billesur secured the brinjals with a knot in the *angochcha*, took out a paisa tucked in the folds of his dhoti and gave it to Ramghulam, who had been waiting with an outstretched hand.

'It will cost you one paisa more,' said Ramghulam.

Billesur smiled and said, 'Would you charge your fellow villagers the same as the market price?'

'You don't come to me daily carrying that angochcha of yours—do you? You must've had a keen craving for brinjals, or perhaps a relative has come visiting you.'

'All right! Collect your money tomorrow. I don't have it on me at the moment.'

Ramghulam had guessed it right. If Billesur ever had a craving for fresh vegetables, he would soak chickpeas and make a curry with oil and spices. Today, he was in the mood for extravagance. On his way back, when Billesur ran into Murli Kahar, the water-bearer, he was quick to instruct him: 'Tomorrow morning, bring me two sers of water chestnuts.' He returned home and knocked on the door, which was opened by the old woman. Lighting a lamp, he milked the goats, set them to graze on the leaves he had collected that morning and went straight to the hearth to make chapattis. Once the sumptuous meal of chapattis, lentil soup, rice, brinjal fry, mango pickle and sweetened goat milk was laid out, he set a sitting plank, placed a glass of water next to it and went to invite the mother-in-law for dinner. 'Amma, come, have food.'

The old woman stood up blushing. Having washed her hands, she walked to the hearth and began eating contentedly. 'I don't see buffaloes around here, but the ghee has a deliciously rich taste, as if made by churning buffalo milk,' she observed while eating.

'Householders must keep a little buffalo ghee handy. Who knows when a guest might come knocking? For my daily use, though, I have goat-milk ghee,' explained Billesur.

Manni's mother-in-law gorged on the food with great relish. Having eaten to her heart's content, she washed her hands, rinsed her mouth and returned to the cot. Billesur retrieved a corn of cardamom from the box of spices, gave it to the old lady as a mouth-freshener and sat down to his own repast. He had not felt such contentment after a meal for many days. Dinner done, he loaned a charpoy from a neighbour, removed the tattered jute rug from the cot to pad up his own bed and rolled out a colourful Bengal mattress for the mother-in-law. A pillow—stitched using worn-out saris that belonged to Sattideen's wife—was also placed to add to her comfort.

The old lady stretched herself on the cot, blissfully closed her eyes and started thinking about Billesur's goats. While Billesur was out buying vegetables from the Kachchi, she had inspected every single goat thoroughly. She counted them and was pleasantly surprised with her own estimate of Billesur's earnings. A herd this size would yield the same profit as rearing three buffaloes. Perhaps a little more.

Billesur was a veritable embodiment of patience. Even though he felt a compelling urge to broach the subject of marriage, not once did he so much as hint at the matter. 'She must be tired. Let her rest today. Tomorrow, she'll bring the subject up herself. She hasn't come all this way just for the heck of it,' thought Billesur.

But before he could fall asleep, he heard faint sobs arising from the other cot. But he stayed still, holding his breath. Gradually, the sobs grew louder, and a clear sound of weeping filled the room. Billesur's was at his wit's end; such misery after a great meal was unfathomable to him. Could this be an indication that the marriage proposal hadn't come through? His heart skipped a beat. Panicking, he asked, 'What's the matter, Amma, why do you cry?'

Crying all the same, the old woman answered, 'I don't know to what strange land your brother took my daughter! Since the day they went away, he hasn't even sent a letter.'

Billesur consoled her. 'Don't cry, Amma. Bhabhi lives in great luxury. Manni Bhaiya takes excellent care of her. They live a little far from the place I had gone to. I often got the news of their well-being. I have been told Manni has found a good job and that he is fully devoted to his wife. Moreover, Bhabhi, too, isn't the little girl you had seen so long ago. They tell me that in two or three years, I'll be blessed with a nephew.'

'May Ram keep them happy! But truth be told, he has betrayed me. I had no one but him to lean on. How I scrape through my days, I alone know,' grumbled the old woman, letting out a deep sigh.

'I am to you the same as Manni was. You stay here with me. There's no dearth of food. Besides, your presence will ensure that I, too, get to eat a proper meal every day,' Billesur pleaded.

Manni's mother-in-law felt happier than ever. She said, 'Son, may you prosper and shine. You're my only support in life. Now that I'm here, I will surely stay on for a few days and take charge of your housework, too. I'm in talks with a family. If everything works out, I shall see to it that your household gets sorted.'

'Nothing could be better than this,' said Billesur, his manliness suddenly awakened.

'Bachcha, I had kept it to me thinking I would tell you when you are at leisure. It seems like a good proposal to me. The girl is intelligent and a good match for you, even though she lacks the good looks of my daughter. The family is a decent one, and the girl can manage your household well enough. So tell me, are you ready?'

'I will abide by your judgement. Whatever agrees with you, agrees with me,' answered Billesur, his voice overflowing with devotion.

The old woman was pleased to hear this. She said, 'Fine, get married, then. She, too, won't have any problem living with you. However, you may have to lend her mother a helping hand. Give her some money before the wedding— not much, only thirty rupees. She is poor and in debt. You may continue to support her afterwards too, for she has no one in the world to call her own. I'll bring the girl to your place. All the ceremonies can be held here itself. If you take the baraat to the girl's place, then you'll have to meet the expenses involved. This may cost you a lot more. But if you hold the wedding here at home, with only a few relatives around, you would be better off.'

Billesur could sense that there was no deception in her words. He said, 'Of course, this is such a noble advice.'

* * *

Manni's mother-in-law stayed on for several days. Eating proper meals, Billesur felt himself grow stronger within 3–4 days. When he urged the old woman to stay on till the wedding, she happily accepted his request.

The entire village was agog with gossip about Billesur. One day, Trilochan cornered Manni's mother-in-law and asked, 'Say, who are you marrying him off to?'

'To one of my relations,' answered the woman.

'And where do they live?' Trilochan demanded to know.

'Why? Are you Billesur?' shot back the mother-in-law, looking him up and down. 'Son, my intentions are honest, and I have no axe to grind. Now tell me this: Who are you to Billesur?'

Trilochan's ploy had failed. He was livid. 'It doesn't matter who I am. You'll learn all that and more after the wedding, once people start shunning Billesur.'

'Even God cannot force a boycott against a man whose relations stand by him. For now, why don't you walk away and start convincing people to shun us?'

Fuming, Trilochan stomped out of the house.

* * *

Life was easy, the days were temperate. Billesur had a bumper crop of shakarkand. On many occasions, he would treat Manni's mother-in-law to a feast of milk and roasted shakarkand. The old woman was as pleased with Billesur as she was upset with Manni. With a feeling of natural affinity, she observed every tree in Billesur's fields, examined the health of each shakarkand plant. Now that she was here, Billesur could go out at night, leaving the goats in her care, and keep a watch over his crop.

On a couple of nights, wild boars raided his field. Twice or thrice, thieves dug up the roots and decamped with the plunder. But the vines hadn't yellowed yet; the crop wasn't ready. Concerned at the losses, Manni's mother-in-law asked Billesur to dig up all the shakarkand and stockpile it at home. Heeding the advice, Billesur piled up the harvest at home, and it was only then that he realized how rich the yield had been. Shakarkand had filled up all every nook and cranny of his home. The mother-in-law, rotund like a shakarkand tuber, smiled and said, 'This will bring in enough money to cover for all the wedding expenses, and yet there would be plenty left for you to eat.'

Billesur looked at the pile, and brimming over with confidence, said, 'Amma, it's all because of your blessings, otherwise, I'm a good-for-nothing.'

The mother-in-law exhaled deeply and said, 'Had my child lived on, he would have been your age, working in the fields just like you. And I wouldn't have drifted about seeking shelter.'

Billesur consoled her and said, 'Call me your son and live without a care in the world. For as long as I breathe, I'll be at your service. You mustn't despair.' The mother-in-law wiped her eyes dry with the *aanchal* of her sari.

Billesur set out for another village, looking for potential buyers for his harvest. He had thought of collecting leaves on the way back. The buyer came the next day, and Billesur traded the lot for seventy rupees. There was complete pandemonium in the village; people were excited and envious in equal measure. Everyone resolved to plant shakarkand the next season.

15

The Importance of Agrasan

The soothing Kartik moonlight danced around. The weather felt mildly cold. Savan birds had flown in from a distant land, turning the twigs of the tamarind tree into their winter refuge. Their noisy chirps rent the air. Sitting on the edge of the *chabootara*, Billesur noticed that Hirani-Hiran, the constellation resembling a pair of lovelorn deer, had disappeared from its usual position. 'The pair goes grazing wherever the pasture is lush,' he muttered to himself. Since those days dew started to fall soon after sunset, Billesur was forced to shorten the leisurely span of his routine stargazing. In fact, the entire village dined early and retired.

That day, Billesur came home early. Manni's mother-in-law, like every other day, had cooked dinner. Lately, he had put on some weight, coddled as he was with the old woman's cooking. Having washed his feet, he stepped into the *chauka*. The old woman laid out his dinner in a thali and slid it gently towards him. To impress her with his pious manners, Billesur had started observing the ritual of setting aside *agrasan*—a morsel saved for animals and birds before one begins to eats. While collecting agrasan, he would hold a little water in his palm and take it thrice around the thali, letting the water drip along the circle. Thereafter, he would repeatedly tap the lota, his eyes shut in a prayer. Once through with his meals, he would pick up the morsel as he left the chauka, keep it aside carefully while washing his hands and then feed it to the goat kids. This admirable rite was performed today in all its glory.

As Billesur ate his dinner, the mother-in-law grinned sheepishly, baring her teeth, and said, 'Bachcha, the month of *Agahan* is set to begin. If you permit me, I would ask for your leave.' She then coughed to clear her throat and added, 'And that other important task awaits us too.'

Billesur swallowed the morsel in his mouth, put on a solemn countenance and answered in a heavy accent, 'Of course, that task needs your attention too.'

'Yes, that's what I meant,' said the old woman. Edging closer to Billesur, she added, 'Do give me some money for the wedding expenses now. The rest you can provide later, two or three days before the wedding.'

Billesur felt jittery at the mention of money. However, being painfully aware there would be no wedding without money exchanging hands, he drew her attention to an obligation, making it the reference point for all further talks. 'Amma, we are yet to consult a pandit on the matter. What if the horoscopes do not match?'

'These are but childish concerns,' rebutted the mother-in-law, her head held high in proud conviction. She added, 'When her character is without blemish, how could the horoscopes not match? Bachcha, the girl is gentle like a cow. And as for her marriage—it would have taken place long back. There was this Ramkhelawan, also a pardes returnee. He was so miserable living by himself that he wanted to run back immediately. And so he came to me with folded hands and pleaded, "Chachi, please get me married. I'm ready to pay whatever you ask." I said, all right, let me see. I convinced the girl's mother and took her horoscope for examination. It was an instant match. Ramkhelawan was willing to pay three hundred to the girl's mother. But then the arrangement came to grief on a question of propriety. The mother said he'd take her daughter to pardes and she would be left here, forgotten and forlorn. "If I take ill, there will be none around to give me a little water. What good is all that money to me?" And so a clinched deal fell through. Then came this Ram Nawaz, zamindar of Chandrapur. His horoscope matched the girl's too. But on the day of *phaldaan*, a relative of the zamindar convinced the mother that Ram Nawaz was a bastard. That was it—the marriage was cancelled right away. Since then, so many decent matches have come her way, yet none worked out.'

Billesur was now convinced the girl was a 'pureblood'. He heaved a sigh of relief. The passionate enthusiasm of Manni's mother-in-law hadn't worn off as yet. Speaking like a sharp-tongued Bengali woman, she added, 'Now, I must share something else with you. Since you're like my own child, I had to tell a hundred lies to make this work.

Or that whore of a mother wouldn't have agreed for you as the groom.'

Irked by the rude revelation, Billesur said, 'But didn't you tell me they are good people?'

'In a manner of speaking, bachcha, we call everyone good. But however good a person might be, nobody wants to lose in a game of dice. Then how could she—the owner of ten *biswa* land—agree to marry her daughter into your family? I had to convince her that you were a Sukul from the illustrious Durgadas clan and that you have earned a fortune working in pardes. "But," I added, "If you demand all the money at one go, it won't happen. He'll pay up, but only bit by bit." Cornered, she relented at last. That's why I've asked you to pay thirty rupees before the wedding.' Saying so, the mother-in-law fixed her expectant gaze on Billesur.

To turn down a proposal financially so attractive would have amounted to sheer stupidity. Billesur said, 'All right, you go ahead tomorrow, with my horoscope and one rupee as earnest payment. I'll come in three–four days and then ask a pandit how well our horoscopes match.'

'Son, you're always welcome at my place. Come as many times as you wish. But whenever you come next, do remember to bring at least fifteen rupees.'

Billesur got up looking solemn and started washing his hands. Her mind at ease, the mother-in-law began eating. After dinner, both lay in their beds, each grappling with their respective conundrum. They did not talk. Engrossed in their thoughts, both drifted into sleep. The mother-in-law woke up early—well before the crack of dawn, while the sky was still studded with fading stars—and began chanting aloud the sacred name of Ram, hoping to wake Billesur up.

The ploy worked; Billesur got up. Rubbing the sleep from his eyes, he asked affectionately, 'Why must you leave so early, Amma?'

Summoning tears to her eyes, Manni's mother-in-law said, 'Son, it won't be wise to delay my departure any further. If I start in the afternoon, it will be dark by the time I reach. I won't get the opportunity to start with the task right away.'

Finding his way around in the dark, Billesur retrieved his horoscope from an old trunk and gave it to the mother-in-law. 'Take care not to lose it,' he urged.

'No, bachcha. Why would I lose it?' said the mother-in-law as she took the horoscope, her manner gleeful and reassuring. Billesur then pulled out a rupee from the fold of his dhoti and placed it on the mother-in-law's palm. 'It isn't much, just a token of care,' he said while touching her feet.

'Did I make any demands of you, child?' exclaimed the mother-in-law. Masking her disappointment over the measly sum handed down to her, she stepped out of the house. Once on the road, she let out a huge sigh of dismay and followed the path leading to her village. Morning had broken.

16

Windfall

Once the mother-in-law was gone, Billesur swiftly wrapped up an important business—he sowed peas in the field where he had previously harvested shakarkand. He had already planted chickpeas in his other field, which, by now, had sprouted high.

But even as he went about all this toil, his anxious mind kept going back to the mother-in-law. The vines of his impending marriage had started to grow buds. Every now and then, he would lose his concentration at work, his breathing would get irregular, and the hairs on his body would stand in excitement.

Finally, the day came when Billesur had to journey to the mother-in-law's village. He milked the goats and stored the milk in a *handi*, an earthen pitcher, securing its mouth with a *muska*. The night before, he had also brought some leaves for his herd to feed on; he served those as well to the goats.

He then fetched water indoors and bathed. Thereafter, he duly set about performing the morning rites, even though he wasn't in the habit of observing them daily. He looked in the mirror while saying his prayers—checking his eyes and eyebrows, puffing and deflating his cheeks, stretching and puckering his lips. Having adorned his forehead with sandalwood paste, he looked once again in the mirror. Widening his eyes, he examined his face closely, trying to assess how sharply the pockmarks showed on his cheeks. He also recited the Gayatri Mantra, though incorrectly, in the hope that it would help him accomplish the task at hand.

Once done praying, he gathered the entire ritual paraphernalia and put it on a shelf in the room. He then ate some stale chapattis. After a quick breakfast, he washed his hands and began to dress for the journey. First, he wrapped his dhoti, taking care its flowing end covered the top of his socks. Then, he put on a kurta and sat on a cot, trying to tie a turban. Once the headgear was ready, he looked again in the mirror, making faces as earlier.

He kept the little mirror in his pocket, threw an angochcha around his neck, topped it with a stole and picked up his lathi. Finally, after wearing his shoes, which had been polished well in advance, he stepped out of his house and put a lock on the door. But before setting out, there was one final custom to be observed: he pressed his nostrils to check which one breathed easier and then stomped his feet thrice on the side of the clearer nostril. Thereafter he picked up the milk pitcher and began walking resolutely, his gaze fixed on the ground beneath his feet.

A little down the road, he caught sight of a pitcher brimming over with water. Billesur felt buoyed by that auspicious sight, as it augured plenitude. The woman carrying the pitcher smiled at him, proud of the good omen she had brought. 'So, when do I get my celebratory sweets?' asked the woman. Billesur assured her with a nod, suggesting that her demand would be met once the task was accomplished, and moved ahead.

He reached the nullah fenced by reeyan creepers and babul trees. Billesur had taken the dusty path that ran along the nullah, on the edge of the pond that belonged to the Baniyas. On seeing him approach, a few cranes flew off to the pond's farther bank. Soon, he reached the Shamsher Gunj crossing, and before long he was at a place teeming with date and palm trees. Next, a vast stretch of green fields, lush with crops, came into view. Dewdrops were aglow with rays of the morning sun, and his eyes were awash with many a colour of the world that flashed and faded before him. He felt his heart tickle with softer sentiments, and his feet moved nimbly. In the euphoria that had filled him, not once did he feel the weight of the pitcher he was carrying in his hands.

The road was lined with mango and mahua trees. When the golden rays of the gentle winter sun passed through them, the entire world appeared wrought in gold. The luxuriant verdure of the trees, big and small, made Billesur feel as if the grey of poverty had faded out of his life. Like a sail swollen by favourable winds, he surged forth towards his destination, confident that the deal to be clinched would bring in dividends beyond measure. As he walked across that verdant carpet, waves of green greeted his eyes as far as he could see. His own heart joined these waves and began to sway in ecstasy. Soon, he could see the houses of the village rise in the distance, towering over the surrounding fields and orchards, giving a concrete form to the happy result he had hoped for all along. Billesur raced ahead with gusto, snaking his way through the winding alleys of the village.

* * *

An old man sat cross-legged on a bathing platform built by the well. Even though he sat facing the sun, soaking in its heat, he shivered as he thumbed his rosary. Up ahead, Billesur saw the house of the village carpenters. It was quite noisy, with the incessant *thak-thak* of the clattery tools busily carving cartwheels. A little ahead was the tailor's shop, crowded with customers. All manner of colourful clothes lay scattered in it, waiting to be snipped to shape and stitched. Billesur caught a glimpse of the tailor too, working diligently on his sewing machine, his head bent in focus. On the other side of the village square, Billesur saw a boy stitching a stuffed quilt. There were two other men beside him, snipping at a new cloth with scissors and setting the pieces up to be sewed by a machine. The marketplace was teeming with people— gossiping, chewing tobacco, spitting, leaning leisurely against their lathis—seemingly smitten by this dazzling array of colours and activities.

But Billesur, unwavering in his focus, marched ahead towards the mother-in-law's house. The crumbling house stood at the end of a cramped alley. Its door was thrown ajar. Billesur stepped inside, calling out loudly to the mother-in-law. The old woman had been cooling her heels at home. The moment Billesur appeared, she rose to her feet to greet him, a smile on her lips, her eyes drawn to the milk handi. Billesur set the handi down with a sense of pride and touched her feet for blessings. The old lady asked after him with touching solicitude, as though they were meeting after ages. She then guided him to a cot and sat herself near him, gazing deep into his eyes. Billesur's eyes betrayed his impatience for marriage.

Having sat quietly for a while, looking solemn, he opened the conversation in a grave manner, like a concerned householder. 'I hope the horoscopes have been examined.' The question set a storm raging in the calm ocean of the mother-in-law's mind. She began narrating everything excitedly—about how she went to a pandit and what the pandit predicted about the forthcoming nuptials—extolling all the flattering details to the skies.

'He arched his brows and said, "She is Lakshmi herself. The moment she sets foot in the house, it'll overflow with riches. The horoscopes match perfectly too. The girl is of the *vaishya varna* and *deva gana*—mercantile in temper and divine in race. And her stars do not disagree with Billesur's."'

The mother-in-law also emphasized that since the girl came from a clan higher than Billesur's, he must declare himself to be of the illustrious Durgadas clan, if not the very lofty Chhanga clan. Otherwise he would be made to feel inferior.

Billesur was on cloud nine. 'Everyone must obey their parents. I have no objection repeating whatever I'm instructed to say,' he assured her.

The mother-in-law heaved a sigh of relief. She then brought a pandit home who was prompt in recommending the match. Billesur accepted the pandit's judgement devoutly. It was decided that the marriage will be solemnized in the coming *lagan*, the auspicious wedding season, and that the ceremonies would be held at the mother-in-law's place. Later that evening, the girl was brought to the mother-in-law's house, and, under the dim light of an earthen lamp, Billesur finally caught a glimpse of his future bride. The sight did not put him off. He was convinced that she had no blemishes, even though he had only managed to peek at her hands and feet. He conversed at length with the girl's mother and, after giving her all manner of assurance, set off for his village. As for the money, he gave it to Manni's mother-in-law.

17

The Legend of Billesur

Billesur returned to his village feeling triumphant, as though he had won a battle and stormed a castle. He moved about proudly, his head raised high. At first people attributed his bearing to the rich harvest of shakarkand. It was only sometime later that the secret surfaced. Alarmed, Trilochan met his closest allies to discuss the emergent matter. During the ensuing discussions, he discovered that this was the very same girl he had asked Billesur to marry. While the revelation made the village widowers and bachelors—the ones older than Billesur—feel sorry about their own marital lives, Trilochan stoked their bitterness further by speaking ill of Billesur. He spoke firmly and announced, 'The girl is a Brahmin, but no one can tell who the father is. After the wedding, Billesur is bound to become an outcast.' Picturing the possibility, the gathering felt comforted.

* * *

Of late, the drummer Doms and the tenants had begun flocking to Billesur, heaping words of flattery on him: 'The house is destined to change and prosper. In a year's time, a son will be born, bringing glory to his forefathers. Earlier, we sighed as we walked past your desolate door, but now we'll stand rooted to the spot and not budge until we're offered some alms.'

Billesur felt tickled with such words, and his wrinkled face lit up with a smile. He imagined himself becoming the tenants' favourite. In spite of his poor finances, he decided to have a lavish wedding, afraid that people might ridicule him otherwise. He knew the tenants wouldn't let this opportunity pass and that if he didn't give them gifts, they would make his social life miserable, nagging him with their unmet demands wherever he went. Moreover, the old bonds of fealty, painstakingly forged by his forefathers, might snap too. He was somehow confident that he would be able to bear the expenses of the wedding.

* * *

Those days, people regularly visited Billesur's house. The barber came every day, demanding to know if Billesur needed his hair oiled or cut. One day, a Kahar came of his own and filled two pitchers of water. A Behna, from the caste of the cotton carders, gave him four balls of cotton for making wicks. The cobbler came asking whether he should fashion the wedding shoes using tender goat skin or ordinary leather. The watchman of the Pasi caste would let out a loud cry daily at midnight, trying to impress Billesur with his diligent vigil. A Brahmin who lived on the banks of the Ganga called on him once and gave two lengths of the sacred thread. Bhattji, the village bard, visited one day, serenading Billesur with songs about Sita's wedding and the devotional poems written by the legendary Braj poet Bhooshan. In short, no one failed to mark their presence in Billesur's court, for he had cast the winning dice. Even the local zamindar visited him at home. That day, the entire village convened to witness the spectacle. The zamindar, of course, had come hoping that since Billesur was getting married, he would make an offering of at least two rupees to the zamindar, as a salutation; and then perhaps the zamindar would ask Billesur if he needed any help with the wedding. The zamindar had also dreamt up other ways of profiting from the event. If Billesur ordered groceries from Kanpur, the zamindar wouldn't just charge him the carting fare but also take a cut on the prices of the goods, as middlemen do.

Trilochan, too, came accompanying the zamindar. He had imagined that by committing himself to the zamindar's schemes with all his strength, he would secure a nibble for himself too. However, on seeing Trilochan, Billesur turned cold. Trilochan and the others counselled Billesur to make a generous offering to the zamindar. He was urged that he shouldn't hesitate when it came to ingratiating even the lord of limitless riches with his humble bit. 'Never go empty-handed to the king, gods and guru,' they stressed, quoting scriptural wisdom in Sanskrit. But Billesur didn't budge. He had nothing but respect to offer. He sat passively throughout the zamindar's visit, as if admitting his helplessness in the matter. After a while, the zamindar left, feeling dejected. Trilochan stuck to him, poisoning his ears against Billesur. He also assured the zamindar that he only needed to drop a hint to the villagers, and they would teach Billesur a lesson.

But the incident had consequences for Billesur; from the very next day, his standing among the villagers improved quite dramatically. To the villagers, the zamindar's visit was proof enough that Billesur had come into possession of a great fortune—nothing less than the fabled treasure of Qaroon, the richest man in Ancient Egypt. The air was rife with rumours of all hues. Someone said, 'He has brought bricks of gold, but he wouldn't tell it to anyone. He is a dark horse. In two years, he'll buy out the entire village.' Another suggested, 'He has stolen jewels from the maharaja of Burdwan, but he hasn't kept them at home. He has buried the loot somewhere, under a garbage heap or perhaps a tree, to keep it safe from thieves.' The more numerous the myths about Billesur, the more respect he commanded. Of late, even those from other villages began greeting him respectfully.

One day, Billesur summoned the village barber and sent him to Manni's mother-in-law in Govardhanpur. The barber was asked to tell her that Billesur would come with a baraat and that she should call the girl to her place because the nuptial mandap would be set up at her house. She was asked to visit Billesur in his village should she need any other details.

Once the barber returned, having relayed Billesur's message, he set out again to invite the relatives. Besides verbally conveying the dates of *tel mayan*—the ritual cleansing with oil and turmeric—and the wedding, he gave each of them a piece of dried turmeric and a betel nut for good omen, as the custom demanded.

Meanwhile, the legend of Billesur's generosity had winged all around. Billesur himself was keen to seize the moment. He went out to borrow a cart for the occasion from the neighbouring village. The cart owner obliged, for the sake of maintaining social relations. Billesur got some wheat flour from the mill and set the village widows—otherwise relieved of routine housework—grinding the lentils. He asked Malkan Teli, the oil seller, to get some sugar from Kanpur. Whatever was left—clothes, goods, etc.—he got the village artisans, peasants, tradesmen and people from other professional castes to arrange them. He sought out the local Julaha, Kachhi, Teli, Tamboli, Dom and Chamar, and got them to pitch in with their bits.* He was also worried about his house; the relatives may not be too happy sharing the space with stinky goats, he feared. But this problem, too, got out of the way. Chaudhary's widow, who lived across the street, eagerly promised to let her entire home—except the room she lived in—be used to accommodate the relatives. And thus, she, too, threw in her lot with Billesur's soaring fortunes.

Soon the relatives began arriving, each one a *manya*, a revered guest—even for Billesur's father—and therefore entitled to cash gifts. When asked to stay at Chaudhary's place, they were suspicious at first, but once they learnt of the goats, they felt glad at being lodged away from them. Picturing the possibility that they would get to sneak away after collecting their gifts—during both baraat and *vidaee*—without having to endure the rituals, many regarded the arrangement to be nothing short of a stroke of luck.

Meanwhile, Billesur approached the village moneylender and borrowed all the jewellery he needed—*kantha* and *mohanmala* to adorn the neck, *bajulla* for the

---

* Julaha is a weaver, while Tamboli is a paan seller.

upper arms, *pahunchi* to grace the wrists and *angoothi* to embellish the fingers. Murli Mahajan, the moneylender, had no objection lending all these to Billesur; he, too, was awed by those legends about Billesur. And as to the jewellery to be given to the bride, Billesur bought them from thieves, paying only two annas for every rupee they cost. He then had all the trinkets cleaned and redesigned. Only the bangles and the anklets were left untouched.

On the day of the tel mayan ceremony, the entire village resounded with the formidable beats of drums played by the Doms. The charm of Billesur's invisible wealth left no one untouched. While returning from the tehsil office, the zamindar of the neighbouring village saw Billesur near the latter's doorway. The zamindar too joined his palms in greeting. With the thoughts of Qaroon's treasure playing on his mind, he struck up a conversation. 'By merely looking at a man's eye,' the zamindar said, 'I can read all the secrets he holds. You're on your way to getting married. Take my horse if you so desire.'

'I'm a poor Brahmin, and I would like to travel like one. But you are our king. You have the means to lavish your subjects with everything,' answered Billesur, careful not to give away too many details.

Sensing Billesur's reluctance, the zamindar smiled and bid him adieu with a *pranam*.

* * *

The day after the Matri Puja, the customary worship of the ancestors, the baraat was set to embark for the wedding destination. The village well was worshipped too. One of Billesur's aunts undertook the job of making the ritual offering of milk to the groom. However, after the ritual, she sat adamantly on the well's parapet, dangling her feet into the well. When asked what caused her to do such a thing, she declared, 'I won't move until I get a gold brick.'

Billesur knew what she meant; he smiled at the delusion she had nurtured, but the villagers thought differently. 'It's a fair demand. After all, for what nobler occasion has he hoarded all that gold,' they argued.

Billesur said, 'Chachi, I'm quite helpless at the moment, as I'm not carrying them on my person. Please pull your legs out safely. I shall give you the brick upon my return.' At this, the villagers turned pale with shock: they were now convinced that the rumours about him were true and that Billesur did possess scores of gold bricks.

The baraat marched ahead. Once it reached its destination, all the nuptial ceremonies—*agwani, dwarchar, byah, bhaat, chota-bada ahaar, bartuni, chaturthi*—were duly observed over four days.* It was the groom who had made all the arrangements. At the end of the rituals, there were just five 'manya' left, still waiting to be honoured with cash gifts. The rest were Kahar, tenants, dependants and people of the village fraternity. Four days later, Billesur came home with his bride. Thereafter, for as long as he lived, he spoke nothing of how he became a rich man.

---

* *Agwani* is the ceremonial welcome a baraat is accorded, while *dwarchar* refers to the custom of worshipping a groom at the entrance of the bride's home. *Bhaat* is the post-wedding feast—usually limited to the kinfolk and partaken of near the nuptial mandap—and *chota-bada ahar* is the wedding feast thrown for the village at large. *Chaturthi* refers to the rituals to be observed on the fourth day after the wedding, which is also the day when the baraat returns with the bride. *Bartauni* refers to the rites observed while setting up and sanctifying the nuptial mandap.

Acknowledgements

I owe a huge debt of gratitude to my editors at Penguin—the very scholarly Moutushi Mukherjee, who commissioned the book and polished its first draft; and the brilliant Vineet Gill, who gave it its final form and was dauntingly meticulous with his interventions. My exceptionally resourceful agent, Kanishka Gupta, is now part of the national publication lore, having steered scores of projects ashore. This book furthers his legend.

By a happy coincidence, Prof. Sumanyu Sathpathy, a celebrated literary critic and translator, was finalizing a project on print cultures around the time I was translating Nirala. He helped me connect the dots and make sense of Nirala's modernity. Scholar and bibliophile extraordinaire Dharmendra Shushant equipped me to read Nirala by giving me words, references and perspectives. My leisurely exchanges with Animesh Mohapatra, a noted translator and a modest marathon runner, helped me develop unsentimental views on the writer. Young Sanskritist Ganesh Tiwari made several obscure references in Nirala's works readily accessible. I am indebted to Dr Vivek Nirala, scholar and grandson of the great poet, Dr Pankaj Chaubey, distinguished Gandhian scholar, and Dr Dilip Choubey, veteran journalist—they remained accessible and forthcoming with resources and references I needed to complete this work. Gratitude is also due to Shaswat Panda, Pawan Chaturvedi, Anandji and Indrajeet Jha. Their friendship affords bouts of creative distraction any translator would deem therapeutic and rejuvenating.

I have to thank my Patna family—Adya, Nita Pathak and Rajnikant Pathak; and my family in Jharkhand—Asha Upadhyay, Prabhash Upadhyay, Abhash Bharadwaj and Divyani. Without their warm company and gastronomical support, literary translations would have felt too dreary. My father, Madhusudan Choubey, has stood by everything I have done ever since I turned twenty. He adds meaning to my endeavours. For that, I am eternally grateful! My wife, Indrani Nilima, a brilliant scientist specializing in high energy physics, can now lecture on Nirala too. Without her gentle, unflinching support, and the emotional cushioning she effortlessly provides, I would have never dared to plunge in the business of books. My mother, Kanti Choubey, was born into a family of literary doyens of Shahabad. Each time a book is published, I miss her sorely but also call to mind the literary inheritance that has fallen to my share because of her.

Scan QR code to access the
Penguin Random House India website